# A DEAL WITH THE DEFENDER

## LOVE ON THE LINE
### BOOK FOUR

## BRENDA ROTHERT

# CHAPTER ONE

Talia

"Want another one?"

The bartender looks at me expectantly, his gaze moving from my empty glass to my face.

I'd love another whiskey sour, followed by three more. Drinking until I flop face-first on the bar sounds fantastic. But I can't, because not spiraling into alcoholism is the one and only thing I've managed to succeed at in the past five months.

"Just some water, please."

He nods and walks away, leaving me to play Tetris on my phone in peace. Today has been hard, and the last thing I need is some stranger trying to strike up a conversation before my dad gets here.

Moving in with my dad at age twenty-five. I definitely didn't have that on my bingo card six months ago. It felt better than I thought it would to sell every piece of furniture I had at my San Francisco apartment, pack up my clothes, and drive to Cleveland.

I never have to look at the leather recliner Kyle used to sit in. Or my bed, where he'd sleep over after we watched *Survivor* and had perfunctory sex.

And best of all, I'll never again step foot in the kitchen where he proposed while I was making his favorite dinner—meat loaf and mashed potatoes. Fuck meat loaf. But not mashed potatoes, because they're delicious.

It was an underwhelming proposal, but did I care? I actually convinced myself it was romantic that my douchebag ex got down on one knee while I was knuckle-deep in two pounds of raw meat, eggs and breadcrumbs. In the video I deleted five months ago, he asked me to turn around, and when I did, both messy hands in the air, he asked me to marry him.

And stupidly, I said yes. If I could go back in time, I'd punch him in the face instead.

"Holy shit, they're here!" the woman sitting on the barstool next to mine gushes. "I told you they hang out here. How do my boobs look?"

"Amazing. But why are they all wearing suits?" one of her friends asks.

The woman beside me responds. "That's what they always wear after games. Oh my god, oh my god, I have no chill."

Games? I narrow my eyes in a glare at my phone screen. It's just my luck that a bunch of pro hockey players would come into the place my dad wanted to meet up with me.

Maybe they play another sport. Any other sport.

"Who's the one with the red tie?" someone asks. "Because he can tie my hands up with that any day of the week."

"That's Carter Stanton," the woman next to me says. "He's married."

"Ugh. Of course."

I glance up, irritation coursing through my veins. It's definitely a group of hockey players. Carter is the captain of the Cleveland Crush, and they had a home game tonight.

If I was feeling nice, I'd warn the woman next to me about the perils of being a puck bunny. Hockey players are users. They change women more often than they change underwear. And screwing them isn't the status symbol puck bunnies think it is.

I'm not feeling nice, though. My vibe has been the same since September—bitter, pissed off and stabby. I haven't talked to anyone but my therapist, my parents, and Sergio, the delivery driver who brought groceries to my apartment. The Chinese and pizza places I ordered from had the decency to leave my food outside the door so I didn't have to talk to them. But Sergio insisted on coming inside to help me unload the groceries. He was the only witness to my steady weight gain, watching the progression from pants with waistbands to stretchy sweatpants.

I'd been living on junk food, only moving from my couch when I absolutely had to. That is, until I ran out of money a few weeks ago.

Dad to the rescue. I would have moved into a homeless shelter before living with my mom. And while my father can be brash and impatient at his job, he's always had a soft spot for his three daughters.

*I promise you this will all make sense one day, Talia. You'll look back and know Kyle did you a favor.*

I crumbled when he said those words to me after the breakup. Then I went for a rage run to a park, where I screamed as loudly as I could until my throat hurt.

Twenty-pounds-lighter Talia was a runner. I ran to manage my moods and my weight, because a love of junk food isn't a new thing for me.

I don't care anymore, though. My weight? Fuck it. Mood? Fuck that, too. When my therapist told me I'm depressed, I just shook my head, because *yeah, obviously.*

"Which one is that?" the woman next to me whisper-hisses to her friends. "He's looking at his phone so I can't see his—" She inhales sharply. "It's Lucien Beaumont. Hot, massive bulge and single. Jackpot."

I sigh dramatically, hoping she might take a hint. She doesn't.

"Ladies, I hope you don't mind," a deep voice says in a playful tone.

I pull the hood of my hoodie up over my head and tug on the strings to tighten it. Lucien continues.

"My buddy is thinking about using a pickup line on a woman, and I told him it's too cheesy. Since you're even more beautiful than she is, I was wondering if you could tell me whether it would work on you."

The woman next to me giggles as I grimace, trying to keep my focus on the game I'm playing. Careless men are picking women up at bars around the world at this very moment, and I can't stop it from happening. I need to stay focused on myself, and where the hell is my dad?

Lucien clears his throat. "Hey girl, is your name Anesthesia? Because you're a knockout."

The three women burst out laughing like it's the funniest thing they've ever heard. I audibly groan, but no one notices.

"I mean, if it was you trying that line on me, it would definitely work," the woman next to me says.

I turn to look at her. She's maybe twenty-one, with long blond hair and an overeager smile.

"You're so familiar to me." She's breathless with excitement now. "Where do I know you from?"

"Are you a model? I did a magazine thing last year and there were some models in it."

She blushes, basking in his compliment. "No, I'm a nursing student."

"If you need to practice mouth-to-mouth, I volunteer." He grins wickedly and she laughs again.

"Are you a hockey fan?" he asks.

"I'm a massive fan. Oh my god, wait ... Are you ... Lucien Beaumont?"

There's a smile in his voice as he replies. "I am. And you are ...?"

"Gullible." I turn on my stool and look Lucien in the eye. "How many times have you picked a woman up with that stupid line?"

His brows shoot up in surprise. One of the blonde's friends, a brunette with bright-red lipstick, glares daggers at me.

"Who invited you into the conversation?"

"I'm trying to look out for her, which you should be doing." I look at the blonde. "You're disposable to him. You deserve someone who isn't picking up a different woman every night."

Lucien is scowling, mentally calling me a cock-blocker. "I'm sorry, who are you? Are you just some random person inserting yourself into other people's business because some guy stood you up?"

I narrow my eyes at him. "No one stood me up."

"Right, because *look at you.*" Red Lipstick sneers at me. "You're wearing a nasty hoodie with a stain on it and you look like you're in the middle of a bender. Instead of being jealous of other women, go take a shower and locate your dignity."

Her words make me recoil, my temper igniting.

"*I'm* the one who needs to locate my dignity?"

"Ladies." Lucien puts his hands out in a calming gesture.

"Now I know what we've been smelling since we got here," Red Lipstick says. "She's living proof that not all incels are men."

"Okay, bitch." I slide off my stool, the flare of anger in my chest the strongest feeling of any kind I've had in months.

"Hey, don't," Lucien says gently, putting a hand on my shoulder to keep me from charging toward Red Lipstick.

"Beaumont, why the hell are you touching my daughter?"

I know that voice very well, but I'm not used to it being so lethally calm. My father, the coach of the

Cleveland Crush, is far more furious than I am right now.

Lucien's hand flies away from me like I'm on fire and he's getting burned.

"Coach, I'm sorry." His swagger is long gone as the apology spills out of him. "I didn't know she was—"

"You're at a bar trying to pick women up? After that piss-poor performance tonight? You should be back at the rink practicing—or sleeping. But instead, you're here touching *my daughter*."

I'd forgotten how much fear Noel Turner instills in his players. He was once a pro hockey player himself, and even though he's forty-seven, I'd still put my money on him in any fight. He's six foot two and he and Lucien are eye to eye.

"I'm sorry," Lucien repeats, a couple of his team-mates coming over to stand behind him. He looks at me. "I'm very sorry."

"Hey, Talia," Carter Stanton says, nodding at me.

"Hi."

I haven't seen him in years, but he's a longtime Crush player, and we've been at the same functions a few times when I was still in college. Since I graduated three years ago, I've been in San Francisco, and I haven't made it back for many games or events.

"This was a misunderstanding, Coach," Carter

says, stepping forward so he's beside Lucien. "Lucy's gonna go home now, right?"

Lucien nods. "That's right. I'm going home, and again, I'm sorry, Coach."

I'm not smiling outwardly, but I'm enjoying his discomfort. A lot.

My dad nods toward the bar's exit. "Get out of here, Beaumont. We'll talk about this at practice tomorrow."

Lucien starts to walk away, the blonde sliding off her stool to follow. He turns to look at her, his eyes wide.

"Who's this, Beaumont?" my dad asks.

"It's, uh ..."

"Kelsey," she supplies, giving my dad a little wave and a smile. "I'm a big fan."

There's a moment of awkward silence as my dad bitches Lucien out with just his expression. I've gotten that look from him before, and it's ... well, terrifying.

"It was nice meeting you, Kelsey," Lucien says. "But I have to go now."

She frowns. "But what about the anesthesia thing? I thought ..."

Carter shoots Lucien a glare. "He's leaving with me. Have a good night, Kelsey."

My dad watches as the two men get their black wool dress coats from the backs of the chairs they were sitting in at the table. Carter leans down to say something to Leo, a player I've only met once, and then they head for the door.

"Let's go somewhere else," I say to my dad.

He nods and waits for me to lead the way. I glance back at the three women and the brunette is giving me the finger. I blow her a kiss and finally allow myself to smile.

# CHAPTER TWO

Lucien

ONCE WE'RE SAFELY outside the bar and away from Turner's fury, I look over at Carter.

"What the hell, man? Coach has another daughter?"

"Two more." He stuffs his hands in his coat pockets to protect them from the bitter January wind. "That's Talia, she's twenty-five, I think. And Audra is like ... two or three years older."

"Damn. He must've had them young."

"You don't know about all that?"

I give him a wide-eyed look. "If I knew, would I have just risked my life by touching his daughter?"

A smile tugs on his lips, now that it's safe for him to be amused about what just happened.

"Coach was an eighteen-year-old rookie when he got his girlfriend pregnant. They got married as soon as they found out. That was Audra, and then they had Talia."

His breath clouds in front of his face as we wait for a stoplight to change so we can cross over to the block we're parked on.

"Even though Coach retired from the Mammoths, he played for the Blaze most of his career."

"Yeah, I know that much."

The light turns and we start crossing the street, Carter continuing with the story. "His wife at the time cheated on him with a guy who played for the Coyotes. It was a bad deal; he was the last to know. So they got divorced and he ended up getting remarried to Angie and having two more kids."

"Holy shit. This would've been useful information."

He scoffs. "Pay fucking attention, man. The rest of us all know."

"Yeah, well, I've only been here for two years. You're the team captain, you should make some kind of informational packet for the rookies."

He rolls his eyes. "If you didn't know Talia

existed, you probably don't know about her and Kyle Macintire, either."

Just the mention of Macintire makes my muscles tense. That smarmy, mouthy fucker is my favorite to fight with during our games against Vancouver. But Carter already knows that.

"What about him?"

We've reached my Range Rover, and I unlock it as Carter talks.

"He and Talia were engaged. They met when Turner coached in Vancouver. Then, earlier this year, every-thing blew up when Kyle cheated on her with Audra."

I gape at him. "Audra as in *her sister*? Coach's other daughter?"

He nods.

"Jesus fuck, like sand through the hourglass."

"Pfft. You know hockey's like that."

"Yeah, I know, but … how did I not hear any of this?"

He huffs out a single note of laughter. "Shit, man. You think any of us are dumb enough to talk about any of it in front of Turner?"

"We hang out, though, outside of work. Like at Isaac's birthday party last week."

He buttons his coat, his nose bright red from the cold. "No one was keeping this from you, Luce. You can be oblivious sometimes."

"Oblivious?"

"Yeah, it means—"

"I know what the fuck it means. I just don't think it's true."

"You know now, so forget it. I haven't seen Talia in years, so I was surprised to see her in there, too."

I shake my head, still off balance from what just happened. One minute, I was securing a cute girl's number, and then I was being cockblocked by my head coach's daughter and reamed by Coach in front of a bar full of people.

The last thing I need is to be on his shit list. We're in a slump, and trade rumors are swirling. I love this team, and surprisingly, I love living in Cleveland, so I need to prove my worth.

"He'll forget about it by tomorrow," Carter assures me, clapping me on the shoulder. "Go get some sleep and I'll see you in the morning."

"Are you going back in?"

"Yeah, Suki and the girls are in Sedona for a spa weekend, so it's one of those rare nights I can go out after a game. I'm not drinking, just having a steak."

"Yeah, I was doing the same."

"Don't worry, we'll make sure yours doesn't go to waste." He grins. "Now get the fuck out of here, Lucy."

"See you tomorrow." I open the door of my car

and get in, trying not to think about the medium-rare New York strip I'm about to miss out on.

Carter heads back and I start my car. It doesn't need to warm up, because I haven't even been here for thirty minutes.

It took me less than half an hour to dig myself a deep hole with Coach. I busted my balls in the game tonight—literally, I tweaked my groin—and then ruined it without even knowing what I was doing.

Hopefully Carter's right, and by practice tomorrow morning, this encounter will be ancient history.

---

"Did I stutter, Beaumont? Get skating."

Carter wasn't right. Coach is bag skating me while the rest of the team watches film from last night's game. My teammates are silent as I leave the group meeting room where we break down games.

"Don't go easy on him," I hear Coach tell our equipment manager, Trace.

Trace is my assigned babysitter while I skate laps as fast as I can. Pros rarely get bag skated unless we have a horrible game. Or talk to one of Coach Turner's daughters, apparently.

Turner's not an asshole, as long as you get him and do what he expects. That's how I knew to humbly exit the meeting to change and skate. Reacting would have gotten me a much worse punishment.

*It's not about fairness. Life's not fair.* Turner says that all the time.

I actually feel for him. Since my drive home last night, I haven't been able to stop thinking about how hard it must be for one of his daughters to have stolen another daughter's fiancé. He's probably extra protective of Talia after all that.

Now I get why she was so angry over me hitting on Kelsey. She probably thinks all men are trash after what Macintire did to her. I don't even know her, but it makes me hate Macintire just a little bit more.

I change into practice clothes, not bothering with pads since I'll be alone on the ice. Trace is sitting on the home team bench at our practice rink when I take off my guards and skate out onto the ice.

It actually feels good to be out here by myself. My dad is a former minor league hockey player, and he got me started in hockey when I was four, making sure I learned skating fundamentals long before I ever touched a stick.

At the time, I hated it. I wanted to be on the ice chasing the puck like all the other kids. But he was right. After a year of just skating almost every day, it was a lot easier for me to execute drills.

He owns a construction business now, but he still drives the Zamboni and coaches youth hockey back home in Duluth, Minnesota.

I lean into a turn, thinking about Talia again. I didn't get to see much of her with the hood of her hoodie pulled tight around her face, but she's pretty clearly still not over what happened with Kyle and her sister.

I wouldn't be over it either. That's some shady shit, doing that to your own sister. Coach doesn't talk about his personal life, but I need to keep up on the high points of it in the future. What a fucking mess I made when I was just trying to prevent a bar fight.

That brunette's shitty comment set Talia off, and she was ready for a fight. No fear at all. I'm known for starting fights over nothing during games. It's a great way to break up the momentum a team may have going.

I like to shift their focus onto me, so at least some of them are thinking more about getting back at me than about scoring. Silas is more of an enforcer, but I hit opponents back sometimes.

Mostly though, I bring chaotic Loki energy into games. I'm a disrupter when I need to be.

It was boxing, which my dad had me train in as a teenager, that taught me not to fear fighting.

Years of taking and throwing punches and

several broken noses later, I see fighting as a skill. It's an asset I bring to my team, just like skating.

About thirty minutes into skating, I'm covered in sweat. I take off the hoodie I'm wearing as a top layer and set it on the half wall in front of our bench as I pass.

"Pick it up, Beaumont," Trace yells, trying to sound authoritative.

"Suck my dick," I call over my shoulder.

He's a good guy, but he's not one of my coaches and I'm not letting him treat me like he is. There's a team hierarchy, and he's not close to the top.

An hour into skating, I'm gassed. I've sweated through the front and back of my T-shirt and I've got swamp ass. We're leaving for a road trip tomorrow—surely Turner doesn't want his top blueliner exhausted.

I won't puke. Some guys puke during bag skates, but I never have. If Turner wants to push me that hard, he's going to wear me down to nothing and I won't be able to play tomorrow.

It's been almost an hour and a half, and I'm fucking wiped and in desperate need of water when Turner walks onto the ice and motions with his hand for me to come over.

Thank fuck. I dig in and skate my fastest to him, making sure the snow my blades throw up doesn't go in his direction.

He passes me a water bottle. I take it, breathing so hard I can't take a drink yet.

"This was mostly about my daughter," he says. "Never, *ever* touch her again."

I nod. "I understand, Coach."

He pinches his brows together and frowns—my cue to shut the fuck up.

"It's also about the other women you were talking to. Goddammit, Beaumont, you're not some nineteen-year-old minor leaguer trying to jump into bed with every woman who's willing. You're a twenty-seven-year-old pro who gets paid a hell of a lot of money to be on this team. Don't fucking embarrass me and the city you represent like that again. Women shouldn't be getting into bar fights over you."

"Yes, Coach."

They weren't fighting over me, but Turner has a short list of what he calls "the last bad idea you'll ever have as a player for me", and one of them is arguing with him. Occasionally, he'll give us permission to challenge him, but it's rare.

"Go watch your film," he says. "Then have Melina work on your legs and feet."

I nod, lifting the water bottle to squirt water in my mouth. Melina's our team trainer, and she's great at massaging overworked legs and feet to keep us from getting too sore.

I take a long drink, downing half of the bottle of water. Sweat drips from my chin and hair onto the ice. I use my soaked T-shirt to wipe my face, and by the time I'm done, my teammates are skating onto the ice for drills.

My teammate Bash smirks at me as he passes.

"You're one stupid motherfucker," he says.

I flip him off, my quads burning with exertion.

"Coach's daughter?" our goalie, Isaac, asks, holding back a laugh. "Really?"

"I didn't know, asshole," I bark. "I'll stick with your mom from now on. Is it weird for you that she calls me daddy?"

"Fuck you, Beaumont."

I skate away from him, too tired for any more verbal sparring. I'll need a nap as soon as I get home today, because our departure time is early tomorrow. Today is my back and shoulders training day, which is a small win. I couldn't do leg day today.

My legs are a little shaky as I leave the ice. Melina will have me switching between the cold plunge pool and the hot tub while I watch my film from last night's game.

Lesson learned, though. I'll never so much as look at one of Turner's daughters again.

# CHAPTER THREE

Talia

THE EARTHY SCENT of brewing coffee pulls me from sleep the next morning. I crack my eyelids open slightly to gauge the time of day. It's not bright yet, but the sun is up.

Dad must drink dark coffee these days, because the smell is powerful even in the upstairs bedroom I'm sleeping in with the door closed. I groan and pull the covers back up to my neck.

"Hey, you're up." My father is leaning against the frame of the door to the room, which is very much open. "Morning." He walks into the room and sets a steaming mug of coffee on my bedside table.

"What?" I croak as I squint against the light, my eyes fully open now. "It's early."

"We're leaving in forty-five minutes. You've got time to shower and pack before breakfast is ready."

I give him a confused look. "I'm not going anywhere."

"You are, though." His voice has a chipper edge to it. "You're coming to work with me."

I hum with amusement. "Oh, is it bring your hot mess daughter to work day? Everyone already knows I'm a disaster, so we can skip that."

He walks over to the other side of the room and opens the blinds, light flooding the room. I protest with a dramatic groan.

"I don't get up this early. Leave me alone."

"Tally, you're welcome to stay with me for as long as you want, but your days of rotting in bed all day are over."

Ugh, this is the last thing I'm up for. My dad thinks he can bring me out of my perpetual bad mood by spending time with me, and he's so far off. What I need is to be left alone.

"I rot on the couch, too," I quip. "Don't worry about me, I'm fine."

"You're not fine."

"Yes, I am," I fire back. "I'm here because I'm broke, not because I need help."

The blinds are open in all three windows of the

room now, and it's like a spotlight being beamed directly at my skull. My father is standing at the foot of the queen-size bed, arms crossed in his trademark *I mean business* pose.

"It's been five months, Tally. I get needing some time after what happened, but enough. You shouldn't have quit your job. It's time for you to focus on something other than your hurt feelings."

I balk at that. "Hurt feelings? Like I was snubbed at someone's dinner party? I'm humiliated. I'd rather take a one-way flight to hell than go to their fucking tropical wedding. Do you know that Audra asked me to be a bridesmaid?"

"I haven't talked to her much lately, so I didn't know that. Let's focus on today. We're leaving for a four-night road trip. Tampa, Phoenix, and Seattle."

I lie back down. "Have a good trip. I'm not going."

I'm pulling the covers back up to my chin when they all fly off me. After pulling them away, my dad drops them to the floor.

"What the hell?" I protest.

"You're coming on the road trip. I don't expect you to be happy about it, but I expect you to go."

"I'm twenty-five years old, Dad. I'm not a teenager you can order around."

He shrugs. "This is for your own good. Get ready."

I laugh bitterly. "No way. I'm not going on a road

trip with your entire team. When you asked me to come stay with you, you didn't mention anything like that. And I haven't even been here twenty-four hours. Let me settle in."

"It's time to join the world again." He looks at the watch on his wrist. "Forty minutes. You can get ready, or I'll carry you from this bed out to my car."

"Good luck with that." I curl up into a ball, cold without my blankets. "I've gotten a lot bigger and you've gotten a lot older since the last time you picked me up."

I close my eyes, ignoring him. He leaves the room and I'm drifting back to sleep before he's all the way down the stairs.

———

I'M ONCE AGAIN PULLED from sleep, but this time I inhale sharply as I'm whisked out of bed.

He's actually doing it. He's going to carry me to his car.

"No! You're going to hurt yourself. Put me down."

"Your old man's not as ancient as you think," he says wryly. "This is for your own good."

"Stop! I haven't even brushed my teeth! I'm in my pajamas. I don't have a bra on."

"Melina's bringing you some clothes, and—"

I have the fingers of my right hand curled around the door frame and I'm holding on for dear life. This is a nightmare. Not only because he wants me to leave the safety of this bedroom for the next four days and nights, but because I still have a shred of pride left. I don't want his team and staff seeing me like this.

With a twist of his shoulders, my fingers fly off the wood doorframe.

"I'll go on the next one, I promise. Don't do this!"

"It's nonnegotiable."

I grab the stairway handrail, holding on so tight my knuckles burn. "No!"

"I tried the easy way." There's a note of strain in his voice as he tries to pull me away from the rail. His tone quickly switches to aggravation. "You want us both falling down these stairs? Let go."

"Don't do this," I beg. "I can't be around people all the time. It's exhausting. It's why I left my job."

He stops pulling. "You're depressed. I get it. Seeing you go through this has been hell."

"Then let me have some peace! You're the one person I thought would have my back."

He huffs a note of unamused laughter. "This is me having your back, Tally. I'm not letting you turn into a bitter old cynic like me."

That gives me pause. He doesn't say much about his divorce from my stepmom, but it had to be hard.

She left him for the contractor who was renovating their home, and he was blindsided by it.

Maybe sincerity will sway him. "I truly don't want to go, Dad. I know I need to get out more, but I want to do it slowly. This is too much."

He shakes his head. "I really am planning to put you to work. You won't just be along for the ride. Contributing to something bigger than yourself is what you need."

I groan. "Don't coach me. Just be my dad."

After a pause, he says, "I am."

He's so damn stubborn. Always has been. I may have gotten a little bit of that trait in addition to my mother's temper.

"Fine," I snap. "Go ahead and embarrass me in front of your team. sounds super therapeutic. But let me brush my teeth and put some clothes on."

He walks back up the stairs and sets my feet back on the floor. "You've got ten minutes."

———

THE CRUSH'S team plane has the team logo on each side. The logo is a scowling Viking-looking man making a tight fist. I guess he's supposed to be crushing something.

I've never been on this plane, but I've been on other team planes with my dad. When I was a teenager, I jumped at the chance to go anywhere and do anything with him. I didn't get to see him much because of his work schedule, but during his offseason, he always prioritized time with me and Audra, including us in vacations with him and Angieand their two kids, and also taking each of us on a trip for alone time with him.

The Crush's plane is a lot like the others. There are fewer seats, and each one is wide and uphol-stered in leather. Some of the seats recline into beds, and there are tables and chairs where players can eat or play card games.

I managed to get a quick shower, brush my teeth, get dressed, and throw a few things into a bag. We rode to the airport in silence, because I'm still in a mood over being forced into this.

"Hey." The team trainer, Melina, gives me a little wave as I'm stuffing my bag into an overhead compartment at the front of the plane, where the coaches and staff sit.

"Hey," I say softly.

I slide into a window seat in an unoccupied row, playing a game on my phone to avoid having to look at or talk to anyone. It's not that I dislike anyone on the team—other than Lucien after last night—but my heart is racing from having my routine upended, and I need to decompress.

It's not even ten minutes before the plane's doors

are being closed to prepare for the flight. My dad stands in the aisle of my row, the players going silent.

"I hope everyone got good sleep last night, because this one's going to be a grind," he says. "Patton's officially on the IR. I want everyone watching their film on this flight. If I catch anyone so much as glancing at social media or pictures of your girlfriend, you'll have my foot so far up your ass you'll be choking on my shoelaces. No fucking around. We need to be laser focused on tonight's game."

There's a low rumble of players saying, "Yes, Coach."

"Also, my daughter Talia is joining us on this trip." He looks over at me. "Stand up and say hi."

Fuck. I shoot him a side-eye glare as I stand, turn, give a weak smile and a one-second wave, and then sit back down.

"She'll be helping out the coaching staff for a while, and I expect everyone to treat her with the same respect you'd give me. She isn't a team employee, but the rules are simple: be nice to her, but don't touch her. Ever."

I bury my face in my hands, mortified. He's acting like I'm a sixteen-year-old virgin.

The "Yes, Coach," refrain is louder this time. I can only imagine how many looks Lucien is getting right now.

He sits down next to me, but I refuse to look at him, focusing on the view of endless runways outside my window instead.

Anytime I or one of my sisters are around one of Dad's teams, it's always been this way. I'm sure it stems, at least in part, from my mom cheating and leaving him for another hockey player.

I didn't know what was going on when it all happened, because I was so young. Now, though, I see how hard that must've been for him. Cheating is the reason I haven't talked to my mom in five months, and the reason things are tense between Dad and Audra.

When Kyle told me he's in love with my sister, Mom took Audra's side, but Dad took mine. And that meant a lot. He could've stayed neutral. Said he loved us equally and we needed to work it out on our own.

He didn't, though. He said she was wrong and he was disappointed in her and wanted nothing to do with Kyle. That meant a lot to me. Not because I'm vindictive, but because it's validation that I didn't deserve what they did to me behind my back.

My dad's been through it twice. I was burned badly enough the first time, though. I'll never expose myself to that kind of heartbreak again.

# CHAPTER FOUR

Lucien

ONCE AGAIN, Talia Turner is glaring at me. But this time it's in the Tampa visiting team training room, where I'm waiting for someone to help me stretch.

"Don't give birth, Beaumont," she says, exasperated. "This is what Melina told me to do."

"Go tell her to find someone else. You're not touching me."

She shakes her head. "I've done this many times. It'll be *me* touching *you*, and it's fine. Now get on your back. Apparently your routine is long, and I'm not missing lunch just because you're a pussy."

My teammate Silas snickers nearby. "Tell him, Talia."

I scowl at him. "Easy for you to say. I want to keep my sac attached to my body. Why don't you touch her?"

He puts his palms up in mock surrender. "I'm not touching her, but if Melina wanted her to stretch me, I'd do it. She's here to help the team."

Talia's scornful hum says otherwise. "I'm here because my dad thinks I'll be happier if I'm contributing to something bigger than myself. But after five months of eating ice cream like it's my job, I'm not sure there is anything bigger than me."

There's a note of amusement in her voice, but Silas and I both give her confused looks.

So she's down on herself. And no wonder, after what that assfuck Macintire did to her.

I lie back, still worried Turner will come into the room and jump on top of me like a pro wrestler over this.

"I just need my back and glutes stretched a little," I say warily. "It'll be quick. And you have to be careful not to push my feet too far."

"Melina told me what you need. And I have a kinesiology degree, so I'm not going to maim you. Unless you piss me off, so don't do that."

A smile tugs at my lips. I can still see her in there —the woman who was ready to fight at the bar last night. But she looked completely different then.

When I first saw her on the bus we took to the

Tampa arena this morning, I did a double take. Without a baggy hoodie tied tight around her face, I can actually see her, and she's pretty. Her dark-blond hair is wavy and it falls just past her shoulders. She has it up in a bun right now, small sections of hair framing her face. Her cheeks have more color. In black leggings and a Crush T-shirt, she really looks like a member of our team staff.

"Left foot," she says, standing at my feet.

I raise my left knee toward my chest and she puts the bottom of my sock-covered foot on her lower stomach. She slowly pushes it forward, stretching my glutes and then my lower back.

I exhale slowly, keeping my gaze on the ceiling.

"Melina said you're adamant about this one, so we'll do it, but no more static stretches after this one. Those are for postgame."

"I know, but I need this one before and after."

"That's fine."

Melina and our goalie, Isaac, come into the training room as Talia is stretching my left side, and Isaac looks like he's got a boulder on his shoulders. He blames himself for our losing streak, and I know he's worried about his position as our starting goalie.

One of our third-line forwards, Grayson Mercado, is waiting for them on the other end of the training room. The floor in here is all a big exercise mat, and it's where we all do pre- and postgame stretching when we play in Tampa.

Carter, lightly riding an exercise bike on one side of the room, groans and stops pedaling.

"Dude." He scowls at Isaac. "Don't do your fart yoga in here. The rest of us shouldn't have to smell your rancid farts."

Isaac shrugs, putting his hands out. "There's nowhere else to do it here."

"Do it in the hallway."

"There aren't any mats there."

Carter gets off the bike and walks over to him. "I think you can handle child's pose on the floor."

Talia lowers my foot back to the floor, meeting my eyes in a quick, concerned look.

"Isaac does fart yoga with Melina before every game," I explain in a low voice. "He likes to get all the gas out of his system because he feels better. He'll do it now and again right before he dresses."

"Oh." Her lips quirk with a smile.

"We're all sharing the training room," Melina says, ending their conversation. "No one has to be as close to his fart fest than me, so suck it up, Stanton."

Carter stalks away, leaving the room. I swear this team is like a family with a bunch of adolescent boys sometimes. We spend more time together than we do with anyone else during the season, so there's a lot of bickering and bitching. And everyone's tense because of our losing streak.

Mercado, who just joined our team this season, recently started doing fart yoga with Isaac and Melina. We got both of them "Fart Yoga Master" T-shirts for Christmas.

"Okay if I lead you through some dynamic stretching now?" Talia asks.

I almost say no. I like my pregame routine. Melina's been trying to talk me into doing the right pregame stretches for a long time. But there's a note of something in Talia's voice that won't let me refuse. I think it's hope.

She looks like a completely different person today. Still surly, but not like she doesn't even have the energy to walk. That's what she looked like last night. Exhausted and defeated.

"Sure, go for it," I say.

She nods. "Okay, let's warm up with some jogging in place."

We both start lightly jogging, and she looks down at her chest, where, if I'm being honest, I was already looking.

"Shit," she says under her breath. "I don't have the right bra on for this."

Her breasts are bouncing up and down, so she puts her arms over her chest to stabilize them. In the moment, I'm disappointed, but it's probably for the best. Turner would choke the life out of me if he saw me ogling his daughter's breasts.

"Those were more manageable before I gained weight," she says lightly.

I don't let myself tell her they're absolutely perfect. She's curvy, and I wouldn't change a thing about her body. I prefer women with softness and a nice, squeezable ass.

After about five minutes, she stops jogging, her cheeks flushed a sexy shade of pink. "Okay, now we'll do some arms. Let's do arm circles."

"So you work in kinesiology?" I ask.

Isaac rips a huge fart, his groan so satisfied it sounds sexual. "Oh yeah, that felt good."

I just shake my head as Talia's lips quirk.

"He does this before every game?" she asks in a hushed voice.

"Every single one."

She widens her eyes in an expression that's half amusement, half disbelief. "I worked at a school for students with physical disabilities before," she says.

Before Kyle Macintire blew up her world. A fresh wave of disgust for that douchebag flares in my chest.

"Guess you know what happened." She's looking away, not meeting my eyes. "Everyone does."

I'm not pressing her on it. After a moment of silence, she says, "Bigger arm circles now. Really control your range of motion, don't just let them fly."

"What did you do there?" I ask.

She gives me a confused look.

"At the school."

"Oh. I was sort of a gym teacher, but it's a private school, so they called me their adaptive physical activities instructor. I made sure every student did some form of exercise every day, and the goal is to make it fun." She drops her arms to her sides and walks over to a weight bench, picking up a bar without weights on it. "You know how to do shoulder pass throughs?"

"Yep." I take the bar and put it out in front of me, not bending my elbows as I raise it up over my head.

"So we did a lot of wheelchair games, like wheelchair hockey and basketball, and relay races, but with things other than running, like you have to roll your chair around obstacles. Music and motion was always really popular with the kids. I did a lot with exercise bands. It's not just about the activity, but also inclusion. Some kids can't really do much, so they would get to participate with someone pushing their chair. I never, ever did anything where the kids pick teams because I hate that with a passion. Someone always ends up last and it's bullshit."

I had observed that she's attractive, but seeing her talk about her work puts it on a whole new level.

She can get worked up—I already knew that—but seeing her get worked up over making sure no kid feels excluded, now that's just fucking hot. Not that I can act on it.

"Is that as far back as you can get it?" she asks as I lower the bar back behind my head.

"Nah, I could get it farther."

"Go as far as you can without causing discomfort."

Another fart tears through the air, Talia laughing this time.

"I get what he's trying to do with fart yoga," she says. "The science is there."

"That's right!" Isaac calls out from his back-down position on the floor, where he has his arms wrapped around his knees to hold them against his chest. "I'm a trailblazer!"

"That pose is called apanasana, and it's very similar to the one you wanted to do when we started," Talia says to me. "It has lots of benefits."

"Smelling Isaac's farts isn't one of them."

"Torso twists," she says, meeting my gaze with an amused gleam in her eyes.

"Morning skate, guys!" one of our assistant trainers, Zack, calls out from the doorway.

"I'm not done with fart yoga," Isaac protests.

"We'll do it again later," Melina says.

"I knew you loved fart yoga," he quips.

"Yeah," she deadpans. "I love it so much."

I have to go change and do the morning skate with my teammates, but I'd rather stay and talk to Talia. I linger as long as I can while everyone else files out of the room.

"Thanks," I say when we're alone. "Let's do this again tomorrow, but build in enough time to do everything you want."

She smiles at me, her expression wry. "I appreciate it, but you don't have to do that."

"Do what? Pregame stretches? You want me to get injured, Turner?"

"You know what I mean. You don't have to make me feel helpful and useful."

I shrug. "I can't help it if you actually are helpful and useful. If you had a fashion design degree, there wouldn't be much you could do here."

One corner of her mouth tilts up in a smile. "Sure. Guess I have to do something, might as well be this."

"Better than fart yoga," I quip.

"Much."

I clear my throat, my expression turning serious. "Hey, I know you probably don't want to talk about it, but Kyle Macintire is a piece of shit and you're much better off without him."

At the mention of his name, she wilts. Her confidence and lightness are gone.

*Good one, Beaumont. You ruined a nice moment.*

"You're right—I don't want to talk about it."

She turns and leaves the room and I sigh heavily, wishing I hadn't said anything about Kyle. I fucked up yet again. Just like I keep fucking up in games.

Even at twenty-seven years old, living my dream of playing in the big league, I don't have my shit together. Not even close.

## CHAPTER FIVE

Talia

LEO SLAMS A TAMPA player into the boards so hard I
can feel the vibrations. They're battling for control
of the puck, shoving and elbowing each other until
Leo manages to hook it with his stick and slide it to
Bash.

It's been a long time since I watched a game from
a glass seat—the front row. I'm so close I can see the
sweat on players' faces. I don't know how my dad
managed to snag me this seat at the last minute at a
visiting team's arena. He may have paid a bundle
for it.

My plan was to hide out in the locker room to
play Tetris and maybe read a book during the game.

I miss my couch back home, where I could hibernate beneath a blanket and truly be alone.

It's only the first day of this road trip and I'm already emotionally worn down. I'm not going to pout over my dad making me come; I know he's trying to help me. Four days of being surrounded by a hockey team twenty hours a day isn't it, though.

Staying with him is temporary. I have to find a job as far away from San Francisco as I can get. One of the reasons I rarely went out after the breakup was my fear of running into Kyle and Audra.

I want to be over it. I want to smile and laugh and live a full life where I don't even think about either of them, ever. Hell, I'd settle for being able to pretend I was living a full life.

I can't, though. Even after months of therapy and seclusion, I still feel like a frayed thread pulled taut, on the edge of snapping. I'm angry. Being betrayed by my sister and my fiancé, the two most important people in my life, cut deep.

Mostly though, I'm hurt. I could never say it out loud, but it's the truth.

The crowd roars to life as Lucien drops his gloves to fight Dimitri Volkov, Tampa's enforcer. Volkov is a rat who slashes when the refs aren't looking. He's paid a bundle in fines for headhunting.

Lucien wastes no time, quickly throwing a hard right hook that rocks Volkov. The fans get even louder, and Volkov jabs Lucien so hard I cringe. My exercise physiology training changed my views on hockey fighting. As the daughter of a coach and former player, I used to cheer for them.

Now that I know how the brain responds to trauma, I know there's nothing to applaud. But it's part of the game, and Lucien seems to relish it. He's grinning at Volkov as they trade a few more hits before Volkov slides and falls to the ice, taking Lucien with him.

The refs break them up, and both men get sent to their respective penalty boxes. Lucien chirps at Volkov as a ref leads him by the elbow to his box. He looks like he's on the verge of laughter.

Volkov, on the other hand, looks ready to commit murder. A dark cloud covers his expression.

Tampa fans pound on the sides and back of Lucien's box with their fists and palms, trying to get a rise out of him. He smiles and waves at them like a queen greeting her subjects, which only eggs them on.

I can't help smiling. He's damn good at what he does, which is firing up opposing teams so they'll focus on him instead of the Crush's offensive lines.

It's working. Carter quickly scores a goal, bringing the score up to 3–0. Isaac's fart yoga must be helping him, because he's chasing a shutout. From the talk I overheard in the locker room earlier, he needs the boost a shutout would give him.

"Miss Turner? May I get you anything?" an arena attendant asks me.

VIP service is part of sitting here, and I've already had popcorn and a glass of wine. I shake my head and smile at the attendant, reaching into my bag for a tip since the game is almost over.

"I'm good, thanks."

She nods her thanks and I return my focus to the game. Tampa's players are getting aggressive, trying to make up for the huge deficit in the score.

When I lived in San Francisco, I volunteered at a group home for disabled adults one evening a week. I led them through modified dance moves to get in some exercise, and then we'd have pizza and an activity, which was sometimes watching a sporting event.

One of the men in the home, Coop, loved watching hockey. I told him my dad coached a team, and I pointed him out on the TV screen during a game. After that, Coop stayed glued to the screen for every minute of the Crush's games and when Dad was on screen, he'd get excited and yell, "That's your dad, Talia!"

I miss Coop. Really, I miss everyone I worked with. I tried to go back to work a week after Kyle called off our engagement, but it was too hard. Some of the children and adults I worked with also had intellectual disabilities, and their reactions to finding out I wasn't getting married were soul crushing.

Many of them didn't understand. They'd ask me questions that made me cry, or offer me hugs and sweet encouragement that made me cry even more. Coop even said he was going to beat Kyle up.

I took a leave of absence from work, and I planned on going back. But with every passing day, week, and month, I drifted further and further from being the person I was before the future I planned was nuked into a mushroom cloud.

Home is safe. Alone is safe. Being here, surrounded by thousands of screaming fans, is jarring, but at least I don't have to socialize with anyone.

I feel the vibration of my phone in my bag, and I take it out to check it. It's an alert I get daily from a countdown app I have.

**Voldemort/Cersei nuptials:** 34 DAYS

I wrinkle my nose and stuff the phone back into my bag. I still don't know what got into me when I told my dad I'd go to the wedding. It felt like a damned if you do, damned if you don't situation.

If I don't go, it sends the message that I'm still upset over the whole thing. Which I am, but I don't want them to know that. Now I face another lousy option, though—going alone and looking pathetic.

It's weird that I haven't found a hot boyfriend while lying on my couch polishing off Ho Hos and binge-watching *Love Is Blind*, but here we are.

My birthday is next month. Maybe my dad will get me an escort for the three-day tropical extravaganza Audra has planned.

Just the thought of asking him makes me laugh out loud. The guy in the seat next to mine side-eyes me, probably wondering if I'm seeing something he doesn't.

I'm going to have to fake a major illness. It's the only option. I'm scrolling through serious but not terminal illnesses on my phone when the buzzer signifying the end of the game sounds.

The home crowd is already filtering out as the Crush players embrace each other, all of them grinning.

The losing streak has been snapped.

———

"STAY out of that last stall, boys," Silas calls as he walks out of the locker room bathroom later. "I just shit a Redwood and clogged it."

I exchange a look with Melina. My dad didn't allow me inside a team's locker room until after I was twenty, and even then, it was only a couple of times, so we could talk in his office when I was in college and home to watch one of his games.

"You'll get used to it," Melina says, shrugging. "They're like cavemen—they communicate with belches and farts and love discussing their bathroom habits."

I'm about to respond when I feel a light, wet spray on my arm and hand. When I turn, I see Bash pointing a bottle of champagne away from himself as he opens it, the foam bubbling over and the liquid shooting out.

"We're drinking it from the bottles tonight, mothafuckas!" he yells. "First drink goes to our badass goalie, Isaac, who got a shutout tonight!"

Isaac, who showered immediately after the game, only wears a towel wrapped around his waist. He's beaming as he takes the bottle from Bash and tips it back, letting the liquid run down his face and chest.

His teammates yell, cheer and clap, everyone relaxed and happy after their win.

When Isaac finishes, he passes the bottle back to Bash, running a hand through his damp hair and grinning.

"Love you guys," he says. "Thanks for never giving up on me."

"You earned this, brother," Carter calls out from the other side of the room.

"And you scored two!" Lucien yells at Carter. "Way to go, Cap!"

Everyone cheers and more bottles of champagne are broken out. Of course, Silas pretends one of the bottles is his dick as it sprays out an arc of thick white foam.

"Did I miss something, boys?"

My dad's voice booms through the room, the celebration immediately dying down.

"Did we just win a championship?" Dad asks, feigning genuine curiosity. "I thought we just won a regular season game, which we should be doing all the time, and you're acting like we just won the cup, the bowl and the series!"

Every player is looking at him, most of them frozen. The champagne flowing from Silas's dick champagne bottle is just a little trickle now.

"I'm fucking with you," Dad says with a grin. "Hell of a game, boys!"

Everyone cheers, the tension lifting immediately.

"But take it easy on the booze," Dad calls as he heads for the visiting coach's office space. "We've got to be game ready tomorrow night."

Our plane will depart for Phoenix in a couple of hours. The equipment staffers have to get everything packed and loaded. If the players are lucky, they'll be able to sleep on the plane and catch a few more hours at the hotel after we arrive.

"Hey, how are you at wrapping and taping?" Melina asks me.

I consider. "It's been a hot second, but I do know how."

"Excellent. Can you help me get some guys taken care of? I desperately need an assistant, but we haven't been able to get the position approved yet."

"Sure, I can help. I won't be as good at it as you are, though."

She waves a hand. "You'll be great. I'd love your help anytime you're up for it."

"Sure, I'll do whatever you need." I follow her toward the training room. "No fart yoga, though."

Her laugh reminds me of my friend Anya's laugh. Anya's still in San Francisco, and we text sometimes, but I haven't been up for much else. Being around Melina makes me think about calling Anya, though. Maybe tomorrow, I will.

# CHAPTER SIX

Lucien

Ten Days Later

"You good, man?" Carter asks me.

I push off the concrete wall in the tunnel outside our locker room, nodding and putting my phone back in my pocket. "Yeah, I was just talking to my sister. She's worried about her follow-up scan next week."

"I can't imagine what that would feel like."

I nod, still gutted over her crying in our conversation just now. Calla still lives in our hometown of Overland, Kansas, but we keep in close contact. She's six months out from beating stage three breast cancer, and she has to get a scan next week to make sure she's still clear.

"She doesn't want to fall apart in front of Matt, but it's okay with me."

He frowns, a crease forming between his brows. "You sure? You look pretty weighed down right now."

One of the equipment interns passes us, rolling a rack of gloves. We both nod at him in greeting.

"Yeah, it's heavy. But the least I can do is listen."

He puts a hand on my shoulder. "You've done more than that."

Not as much as I would have liked to do. I was seventeen, and Calla was twenty, when we lost our mom to breast cancer. Then that bitch of a disease came for my sister, and it stole almost everything from her.

I made sure she and my brother-in-law were taken care of financially, and I paid off their house to lift some of the burden, but that's just money. I stayed with them for a month of my offseason so I could be there for her last month of treatment, and it was the hardest thing I've ever done. Harder even than watching Mom wither and die, because I knew how wrecked Mom would be over Calla going through it.

I take a deep breath and roll my shoulders. "Gotta let it go for now and get into game mode."

"Come on, let's go eat."

We just got back from a road trip yesterday, and we have a home game tonight. When we walk into our team dining room, the savory scent of grilled steak makes my stomach rumble.

Our team chef, Marco, has the usual pregame buffet set up. He's standing behind a grill at the end of the buffet, where he prepares grilled steak and chicken to order, so it's still steaming when he puts it on our plates.

"Hey Marco," I say as I pick up a plate. "Looks great."

"Steak medium rare," he says, gesturing toward a sizzling steak on his grill. "And grilled chicken for you, Cap."

Marco is all business during mealtime. He's a tall, wiry guy who shaves his head completely bald. He rolls through assistants because he's impatient and doesn't tolerate mistakes.

"The soup is butternut squash and carrot with a bit of coconut cream," he says.

"I'll take a little."

He ladles about a fourth of a cup into a bowl and passes it to me. I don't like to eat much soup on game days because it weighs me down, but a little bit is okay.

I thank him and go to the salad bar while my steak finishes cooking, getting half a baked potato and making a salad. Puck drop is still four hours away, so it's time to fuel up with carbs and a little protein.

Once I have my steak, I scan the small dining room for an open seat.

Talia and Melina are sitting together, smiling and talking. Those two have become tight since Talia started traveling with us. An invisible tug pulls me over to their table.

"You mind, ladies?" I ask.

Talia tips her chin, her hazel eyes meeting mine. I study them for just a second, trying to decipher something. Anything.

Our pregame stretching routine has become a ritual I look forward to. Since she started traveling with us, we haven't lost a single game. She froze me out for a few days after I mentioned Kyle, but she's since warmed back up.

I'm not sure how tonight will be for her, though, because we're playing Vancouver—Kyle's team.

"Sit down, Beaumont," Melina says. "We're talking about our periods."

I put my tray down across from Talia's and sit, my lips pulling up in a grin. "I've actually got major cramps today, they're the worst."

"You have no idea," Talia says lightly.

"I always figured they were like shit cramps."

Both women scoff.

"Yeah, no," Melina says. "You can't shit out your period and make the cramps go away."

"How's the ankle?" Talia asks.

I tweaked my right ankle a couple days ago and she's been wrapping it. Sometimes her fingertips will trail over my bare skin for just a little bit while she's doing it, and just that contact makes my dick twitch with awareness.

The more I'm around her, the more I want to be around her. She's usually cryptic, careful with what she says and how she says it. But occasionally, I get glances at the fire that seems to always be simmering beneath the surface.

"Ankle's good. You haven't been watching *Severance* without me, have you?"

Her lips quirk. "Nope. But we need to watch the next one today, so work it into your busy schedule."

"Hey, tomorrow's an off day. We could always just binge the rest of it."

Melina clears her throat—probably reminding me how dangerous it would be to spend time off with Turner's daughter. I can't help it, though.

"Maybe," Talia says.

She's nibbling on an omelet, and I wonder if she ate anything else before I got her. I don't like her digs at herself over her weight and appearance.

"You want some steak?" I offer.

"No, thanks."

"Hey, can I sit?" our backup goalie Preston Smith asks.

"Of course," Melina says.

My gaze locks onto Talia's again, and I think I see a note of playfulness there.

"Does anyone have time to stretch me before the game?" Preston asks Melina.

"Talia might be able to."

A jab of aggravation hits me out of nowhere. Preston looks like a fucking male model. He's been in fashion magazines, and a photo of him getting out of a pool wearing nothing but underwear went viral not long ago, with women thirsting over him.

"She'll be busy stretching me," I say, my tone authoritative.

There's a moment of awkward silence before Talia says, "You can join us, though. It's not like it's a private thing."

She's looking at me as she says it. I play it cool, spending more time than I need to cutting my next bite of steak.

"You cool with that?" Preston asks me.

"Yeah, whatever."

I'm caught off guard by my reaction to Talia telling him it was okay. I've been in a groove since our first stretching session together. She's my lucky charm, and I don't want to share her.

It's not like I can say that, though. I have to pretend I don't care.

———

"TRUNK TWISTS," Talia says, avoiding my eyes. "Control your movements and get full range of motion."

The closer we get to puck drop, the more she's shut down. Preston is oblivious, standing a few feet away from me and following along with our stretching routine.

She doesn't even quirk a smile over Isaac's fart yoga today. That's unlike her.

It's because of Macintire. She probably hasn't had to look at his ugly fucking face since they broke up, and she knows he'll be out on the ice tonight.

Usually we have light conversation while we stretch, but not tonight. She's all business.

"Hey, Talia, I gave Suki your number," Carter says as he walks past us. "Prepare yourself, she wants you to go out with her and Mara and Lainey. You get those three together and it's a lot."

There's affection in his tone. Carter's wife is the counterbalance to his gruffness. And he's actually not that gruff once you get to know him. He's just not a smiler.

"You need to meet their pig," I say.

Talia arches her brows in question. "Their what now?"

"They have a pet pig. Darling."

Her lips shift into an almost smile. "Darling?"

"One of their girls named him."

"I love that. Is he one of those micro pigs?"

Carter's note of laughter from an exercise bike along the wall is unamused. "If three hundred and fifty-two pounds is micro, then yeah."

Talia's eyes shift to mine, alight now. "For real?"

"It's Leo's fault," Carter grouses. "He had one job."

"Leo thought it was a micro pig, but it wasn't," I explain. "It was a gift to the girls and by the time they realized he was growing into a full-size hog, they all loved him too much to give him up."

"I didn't!" Carter calls out as he pedals.

"Bullshit," I mutter. "He loves Darling."

Her light mood quickly vanishes, and she cuts the stretching routine short, making an excuse about needing to help Melina with something.

I finish stretching with a foam roller on my own, Metallica playing over the locker room speakers. This is when lots of us want to be left alone, so we can get in the right mental zone.

I'm a visualizer, but tonight, instead of visualizing myself getting to the puck first and upsetting Vancouver's offense, I'm picturing myself beating Macintire's ass. I'm holding the collar of his sweater, standing while he's on his knees, and I hit him over and over. My hands don't even hurt. All I can see is his tortured expression as I break his face open.

I try to shake it off because I need to have a clear, focused mindset going into this game. I need to be in control.

On-ice warm-ups will start soon. I should sit somewhere alone and do some breathing exercises to calm myself, but fuck that. I'm going to find Talia.

She's not in the locker room, and when I check Coach's office, she's not there either. I'm starting to wonder if she left when I glance into the equipment room.

She's standing in the corner, her arms wrapped around herself and her head down. When she hears me come in, she looks up, her eyes wide, tears streaking down her cheeks.

"Hey," I say softly.

She sniffs and stands up straight. "Hey, I just came in to grab something for Melina."

"Yeah? What?"

She looks side to side. "Well ... she needed more tape. I don't see any in here."

I close the door to the room and walk over to her, my skate blades tapping on the concrete floor.

"You don't have to pretend. Macintire's a worthless piece of shit. He's not worth a single tear from you."

Her eyes flood again.

"I know. I mean, I know I *should* know. I want to be able to watch this game like a badass bitch who doesn't give a single fuck about him, but ..."

"It's hard."

She nods. "I said I'd go to their stupid fucking wedding next month, but like ... how?" Her voice breaks with emotion. "I'll just cry and hide in the corner the whole time."

I drop my brows. "Fuck them and their wedding. Why would you put yourself through that?"

She shrugs. "If I skip it, it seems like I'm not over it, and if I don't skip it ..." She laughs as a tear trails down her cheek. "I prove I'm not over it, I guess?"

I can't miss pregame warm-ups. But I also can't leave this conversation.

Gloves tucked under one arm, I reach out with my free one and brush my thumb over the tear. Her eyes widen as she holds my gaze.

"Just get through tonight. You're a beautiful, strong woman and he's a piece of shit. If it's hard to be in the same building as him, grab an Uber and go home. Get some ice cream. Buy yourself something you really want."

Her shoulders drop with a deep exhale. "Yeah,

that's ... not a bad idea. I want to be able to sit in the stands and look like I don't care, but ..."

"You're not a soulless sack of shit like him, and you do care. It's nothing to be ashamed of."

A corner of her lips quirks into a smile. "Are you just really good at pep talks?"

"I'm not bad, but I also know Macintire. We used to play on the same team. I fucking hate him."

"Why?"

I shift on my feet, nervous the locker room is empty out there. "Long story, and I have to hit the ice. Text me if you want to watch *Severance* later."

"You want to come over to my dad's?"

I balk. "He'd love that. I meant we can watch them at the same time. Me at my house and you at yours."

"Oh."

Was that flicker on her face disappointment?

She nods. "Yeah, that sounds good, actually. I don't think I have your number, though."

"I'll get yours from Melina."

"Beaumont?"

The yell in the locker room means I'm missing warm-ups. I head for the door, looking over my shoulder at Talia.

"Catch the game if you can. I think you'll enjoy it."

# CHAPTER SEVEN

Talia

LUCIEN SWIPES A HAND across his mouth, wiping away the blood running from his nose. I haven't been able to look away from this game since I got to my dad's house and turned it on.

The first minute Lucien and Kyle were on the ice at the same time, Lucien was chirping at him. He's been relentless, flying toward Kyle every time he starts a shift. He's in the penalty box for the third time tonight, and every fight has been against Kyle.

I shouldn't like it, but I do. It feels damn good to see Lucien pounding on my horrible ex. Kyle's a little shorter than Lucien's six foot two, but he's much leaner. Lucien is dominating him.

D-men don't usually have lightning-fast reflexes, but Lucien does. He bobs and weaves like a boxer. He's fast and fearless. I've never seen anyone take the punches he can without reacting.

"Beaumont seems to be trying to get thrown out of this game," one of the TV announcers says.

"This is what he brings to his team, John," the other one says. "He calls it Loki energy. Beaumont is like a plane nose-diving into the opponents' offense."

They think this is just Lucien being Lucien. I would've thought the same if he hadn't made that last comment to me about enjoying the game.

He's doing this for me. I never want to be involved with a hockey player again, because once was more than enough. But it's sexy as hell that Lucien is trying to make me feel better. Taking body shots and actually bleeding over me.

Kyle had to go to the locker room after that last fight—probably to get stitched up. The game is tied 2–2, and even though I've seen my dad yelling at him when the camera cuts to the bench, Lucien is on a mission.

When they show a view of him sitting in the penalty box, it feels like he's looking right at me.

*You're a beautiful, strong woman.*

No one but my parents has ever called me beautiful. Kyle and I were both drunk the first time we slept together, and we just kind of kept doing it. I never felt like we fell in love exactly; we just became close friends who also fucked. There was no wooing.

When Lucien wiped my tear away earlier, I got a flutter. I didn't want anyone to see me crying over Kyle, but he made me feel like it was okay. Understandable.

This morning, my dad asked me if I wanted to stay home today. He didn't even have to say why he was asking—we both knew. I didn't want him to know I was bothered by the thought of seeing Kyle, so I told him I wanted to go.

I like my new routine of helping him and his team out. I assist Melina, stretch Lucien before and sometimes after games, and help Marco in the kitchen when he lets me.

He taught me how to make an omelet, and now I make them for my dad and me all the time. It feels good to be great at something, even if it's something small and simple like making an omelet.

On a commercial break, I walk into the kitchen and grab a snack. Pistachios, because there's not much junk food here. We grab ice cream from a local place a couple times a week, though. Dad's not against junk, he's just not home much to need groceries.

When I'm back on the couch, a comfy blanket on my lap and the game back on, a text comes in on my phone.

*Audra: I heard you're living with Dad now. That's great.*

My heart pounds as I read the message a second time. Is she being passive-aggressive? I can't tell. She might be at the arena right now, watching the game.

We used to be close. We talked several times a week and met up for brunch every Sunday. I often wonder which brunch it was that I sat across from her, happily chattering and sipping a mimosa, while she knew she'd just fucked my boyfriend.

It had been going on "for a while", Kyle said when he told me about him and Audra the night he broke things off with me. He didn't believe in marriage, he reminded me, and he'd changed his mind about being tied down to just one woman.

Three months later, he and Audra announced their engagement. That cut me even deeper than the cheating. I was with him for two years and he said he was adamantly opposed to marriage the whole time.

Guess he was only opposed to marrying me. I know I'm better off without him, but it still hurts. If it had been anyone but Audra, it wouldn't have been so completely crushing.

I put my phone face down on the couch cushion next to me, returning my attention to the game. I haven't responded to any of Audra's texts since I confronted her about Kyle, and I don't plan to start now.

I made a fool of myself that day. I went into her apartment full of rage, planning to unleash my fury on her. That didn't last long, though. I ended up bawling my eyes out and asking her why. And how. And where.

She flinched, like the questions were hurting *her*. Such irony. I don't hate her, but a betrayal like that isn't something I can overlook. My therapist told me I should forgive her for me, not for her, but I'm not ready.

Vancouver scores and I yell at the TV. I've always rooted for my dad's teams, but now that I've gotten to know his players better—especially one in particular—I'm fully invested in every game.

---

*Lucien: Our outies should meet. Want to get lunch and watch our show?*

I smile as I read the text. I'd love to say yes, but I can't.

"This color will be fabulous on you," Suki's friend Mara says, holding up a sleeveless blue dress on a hanger.

"Okay, I'll try it on," I say as I type out a reply.

*Talia: I'm shopping with Suki and Mara. Then we're getting manicures and going to a sushi place. Raincheck?*

Three dots appear on my screen as he replies.

*Lucien: Definitely. Have fun.*

"Nothing says living your best life like red, though," Suki says, holding another dress up.

Carter's wife texted me this morning and asked if I wanted to join her and her friend for the day. My dad practically begged me to go, shoving his credit card into my bag and shooing me out the door. I was groggy after a late night of watching two episodes of our show while texting Lucien about it, but after an iced coffee, I'm wide awake and having a great time.

"I don't know if I can do this," I say, sighing.

"What, find a dress?" Mara asks. "We've got you, girl."

"No, the wedding. I don't want to go. Why should I force myself to go just because I care what they think? It's not just one afternoon, it's three full days. Trapped on an island with them."

Suki pauses from scanning the dress racks at the Nordstrom we're at, looking at me.

"You don't have to go. I couldn't smile through that bullshit."

Mara hums her disapproval. "I'd spend my last dollar getting my hair and nails done and show up there with the hottest man I could find. I wouldn't stop smiling once the entire three days. Does that make me petty?"

"Well, along with every other thought you've ever had, yes," Suki says, returning to the rack.

I like them both a lot. From the time they picked me up from my dad's house, they've treated me like a longtime friend. When Mara said she needed to go dress shopping, I told her I did, too, and when I told them why, they were blown away.

"Okay, hear me out." Mara holds up a short, strapless ivory dress. "You get your tan on and wear this little number."

Suki grins her agreement. "Yes, girl. I mean, not just the *fuck you I'm wearing white* part, but the dress itself. That fabric is delicious."

"Delicious on a Kardashian, but I can't pull that off," I say.

Mara pulls her brows together. "Of course you can. Your boobs will look amazing. At least try it on."

"How much is it?"

"I'll buy it for you," Suki says, waving a hand.

She's so freaking sweet. I give her an appreciative look. "No, my dad said to spend as much as I want. I was just looking for an excuse to wear a tarp instead."

Mara barks out a laugh. "Text your dad right now and ask him to adopt me." She comes over and holds the dress up to me.

Suki inhales sharply. "Yes. It's divine."

"I don't even know if I'm going," I protest.

Mara arches a brow. "If you don't, you'll have a fabulous dress in your closet for another time."

"I'm thinking strappy gold shoes," Suki says. "Are you going solo or with a date?"

I sigh softly. "Solo."

Mara shakes her head. "No, you're not. You need an emotional support fuckboy. I'll ask Leo which of his teammates is single and we'll tell you which one is the most tolerable."

"He has to be hot, too, though," Suki says.

"True."

I pick up a flowered, floor-length dress, holding it up. "What about—"

"No." Mara vetoes it after a glance, then looks back to Suki. "Crawford?"

Suki wrinkles her nose. "Well, he's single ..." She considers. "What about Lucien?"

Mara lights up. "Yes. He's a good guy, right?"

"Carter's never said anything bad about him. And he's free during the break."

The wedding is during the pro hockey all-star break in February. Kyle knew when they set the date that he wouldn't be a contender for the all-star team.

"I can't believe they snubbed Lucien," I say. "He should have made the team."

Mara gives me a mischievous smile. "So comfort him. Ride him so hard you can't walk straight at the wedding."

My cheeks heat as I try to laugh the idea off. "I

hardly even know him. And I'm sure he already has plans for the break."

"Ask him," Suki says.

I shake my head. "You guys, I don't know if I'm even going."

"Okay, forget about that for now and try these on," Mara says.

I figured I should go up a dress size since my casual clothes fit tighter these days. Mara and Suki both have lean, perfect bodies. But I don't want to be a baby, so I go into a fitting room and put on the red dress.

My boobs are like grapefruits. They fill the dress and then some. My waist is thicker than it used to be and my arms are bigger. I just want to put my leggings and baggy hoodie back on.

"Let's see, Talia," Suki says.

I groan. "Don't make me."

"Get out here, ho!" Mara barks.

The woman in the dressing room next to me gasps, shocked. I smile as I open the dressing room door, not stepping out but letting them see me in the dress.

"It's so pretty on you," Suki says.

"That one's a definite yes," Mara says. "You're going to need more than one dress if this shitshow is three days long. Let's see the white one."

I give them a pleading look. "I can't wear that."

"This is just a try-on," Suki says. "No commitment."

I groan and close the dressing room door. I've never worn a strapless dress in my life, and it seems like a horrible idea to try one on for the first time when I look and feel like the Pillsbury Doughboy.

*Let's get this over with.*

I take the red dress off and put the ivory one on, unable to zip it all the way in the back. When I open the door a crack and say, "It's a no, it won't zip all the way", Suki and Mara push their way into the dressing room, which isn't exactly huge.

"Let me try to zip it," Suki says.

"You'll break the zipper. I'm too fat for it."

"Bullshit," Mara says. "I'd pay so much money to have your boobs. I'd lube those babies up with oil every night for my man."

The woman in the room next to us scoffs with disgust. Mara smirks.

I feel the zipper slide up, locking me into the formfitting dress.

"It's so gorgeous on you," Mara says.

I'm wearing my regular bra, so it looks weird. The sheer ivory material washes me out right now, but like Mara said, with a spray tan ...

"It's not bad," I say weakly.

"Not bad?" Suki gathers my hair at my neck and holds it up at the crown of my head. "You look like a queen. With a tan, your hair up, and some jewelry, every man's jaw will drop when they see you."

"I've gained some weight, though, and—"

"Well, it went to all the right places," Mara says. "This is the dress and Lucien is the guy."

I crinkle my brow. "Okay, I'll get the dress, but I still don't know if I'm even going. Don't say anything to Carter and Leo, okay?"

"We'd never do that to you," Suki promises. "Do you want to try on the blue dress, too?"

I shake my head. "I'll buy the red and white ones. Then let's go check out the shoe section."

Suki and Mara leave the dressing room and I glance in the mirror again. I don't even look like myself in this dress. I look like Mara—a bold, confident woman who takes no shit.

I'm not, of course. But Kyle and Audra don't have to know that. I just have to *look* like I'm thriving. And it would be a lot easier with a date.

I'd rather chew on broken glass than ask Lucien to be my pity date. Maybe I'll just show up for the wedding and skip the rest of the festivities.

Yes, I can show up for the ceremony and then return to the comfort of my room at my dad's. I'll spend the rest of the break with my dear friend Little Debbie.

CHAPTER EIGHT

Lucien

I BRUSH the snowflakes from my hair and ring Carter and Suki's doorbell. A few seconds later, their pig Darling looks at me through the sidelight windows beside the door, pressing his nose to the glass.

Carter opens the door and frowns at the pig. "Get out of the way, Darling."

Their pet moves farther into the doorway, completely blocking my entrance as he snuffles at my feet and legs.

"Hey, big guy." I pet his head and scratch his ears like he's a dog.

He's wearing a Cleveland Crush sweater, his bulk stretching the letters out. Suki has all kinds of custom clothes made for him to wear in winter when it's cold, but he still has to go outside to do his business.

"Hallie, call Darling!" Carter calls over his shoulder.

"Darling!" his youngest niece yells. "Come here, my Darling!"

The pig looks up at me with a glance that says, *You understand, don't you?* before turning to trot away.

"Come on in," Carter says. "We're watching football. Harry's helping the girls bake me a birthday cake."

I step into the house, which smells like chocolate. Suki's good friend Harry is a chef. Their home is a hub of sorts for their friends and family. Suki loves to host, and as the wife of our team captain, she plans and hosts a lot of informal get-togethers in their home.

"Thanks for the invite," I say, taking my boots off and putting them on the big rug next to the door.

"Glad you could come."

He leads the way into the two-story family room, where the game is on. Bash and Lainey are sitting in an oversized chair, her on his lap and a blanket covering both of them. Leo is sitting on the massive sectional, Talia and his wife, Mara, on the other side of it, both looking at something on Talia's phone.

Talia meets my gaze and smiles. I woke up thinking about that smile this morning.

"Hey," I say, giving a general wave to everyone saying hi to me.

"You know where everything is, help yourself," Carter says as he sits down in a leather recliner.

"No fucking way that was holding!" Leo cries. "These refs are on the take."

"Hey, Lucien," Suki calls out. "Want a drink?"

I walk into the kitchen, where Suki is drying a dish and Olivia, Charlotte and Hallie are all watching Harry pipe frosting onto a three-tier cake.

"I'll get it," I say. "I figured you guys would shop all day."

She shrugs. "We were hungry, and then the roads were getting bad, so we decided to come home."

Her hair is up in a loose bun and she's wearing leggings and an Ohio sweatshirt. She and Carter had a whirlwind start to their relationship. It started back when she was working as his nanny after he got custody of his sister's three daughters when she passed away. Now it feels like they've been together forever.

"That cake for me?" I ask the girls.

"No, but you can have some," Hallie says. "It has a chocolate cake, a white cake, and a chocolate chip cake."

"Nice."

"Like I said, make sure you get pictures as soon as it's done," Suki says. "We have an accident-prone pig on the loose."

"Hey Harry," I say to the tall, lean man holding a bag of frosting with a tip up to the cake.

"Hi, Lucien. How's it going?"

"Not bad. Good to have a day off. How's the restaurant?"

"Busy. But that's a good thing."

"Can we go sledding?" Charlotte, the middle girl, asks me.

They still remember the time Leo, Isaac and I took them out on a day off last season so Carter and Suki could have some time alone. We went sledding, had burgers and shakes at a place that stuck all kinds of cakes and candy on top of the milkshakes, and played arcade games for hours.

I spent more than three hundred bucks on arcade tokens, and it was worth every penny for the big stuffed unicorn we all pooled our tickets to get for Hallie.

"Yeah, I'd be down for sledding," I say.

"Okay, the hard part is done," Harry says, handing the bag of light-blue frosting to Olivia. "Now you can write something."

"What should I write?"

"Happy Birthday," Charlotte says, her tone implying it's obvious.

"I don't know if I can fit that. I'll try."

"Luce, bring me another beer!" Leo calls from the living room.

"Do I look like your wife?"

"No, you did not," Mara calls out.

They aren't married yet, but she doesn't let jokes like that slide.

When I walk back into the living room, Talia's eyes find mine again, and she's fighting a smile. "You two do have similar hair."

"Anyone else want one?" I ask.

"I'll take a gin and tonic," Mara says. "With generous ice and a lime wedge, please."

I scoff, though I'm not at all offended. "So I'm the bartender?"

"Don't worry, I tip well," Mara says.

"You want anything, Talia?" I ask.

"We should do boozy milkshakes!" Suki says.

"I want a boozy milkshake." Hallie forgets the cake decorating.

"Just a regular milkshake for you, Hals," Suki said.

Talia gets up from the couch. "I happen to make the world's most incredible spiked chocolate milkshakes. If you don't have all the stuff, I'll go grab what we need."

She's wearing dark-gray leggings today, with a lightweight black sweater. Her hair is loose around her shoulders. When she walks into the kitchen, I follow.

"How'd the shopping go?" I ask as she makes a list of ingredients.

"I survived," she quips.

"You more than survived." Mara walks into the room and puts an arm around her. "You have two gorgeous dresses for Lucifer's wedding. All you need now is a date."

Talia's cheeks turn pink as she flicks a glance at me and says, "I don't mind going by myself."

"You're going to a wedding?" I ask.

"Kyle and Audra's."

I just look at her for a second, because I can't believe what I just heard. She's going to the wedding of the man who cheated on her? Probably because it's also her sister's wedding, but she's well within her rights to flip those two assholes the double bird and skip it. With all these people around, though, I don't say that.

"It's over the all-star break," Suki says. "So she just needs to find a man who's free over the break and wants to hang out in Hawaii for three days."

Talia gives Suki a look that wordlessly says, *Shut up.*

"I'll go with you," I offer.

"Perfect!" Suki claps her hands together, looking

up from Talia's grocery list. "I have everything we need except whipped cream."

"We know why you're out of whipped cream, pervs," Bash quips from the other room.

Talia's face is a darker shade of pink now, but I don't know why.

"You don't have to do that, Lucien," she says. "Really, I'll be fine."

"Are you kidding? I'd love to go with you. I can't stand Kyle. We can sneak Nair into his shampoo. It'll be fun."

She looks flustered. "I don't even know for sure if I'm going."

"Well, if you decide to, I'm in."

"I'll go get some whipped cream." She won't meet my eyes, and I don't know why she's acting so strange.

"I'll come with you."

I haven't even taken my coat off yet, and this will give me a chance to talk to her about why she doesn't want me to come with her to the wedding.

Once we're in my car, before I've even started it, I look over at her.

"It felt like you were uncomfortable back there. Is there someone else you want to ask to go to the wedding with you?"

She shrugs. "No. I'm just uncomfortable over the whole thing. If I don't go, everyone will think I'm at home crying over it. If I go alone, I'm pathetic. If I go with you, they'll wonder how a chunk like me got a date like you and assume it's a pity date. I can't win."

I gape at her in disbelief. "If you don't want to go, don't. You don't owe them shit, Talia. And don't put yourself down like that. I don't like it when people say shit about my friends."

A smile tugs on her lips. "Are we friends?"

"I think so."

"Even though I cockblocked you?"

I shouldn't say it. She's Turner's daughter. Forbidden fruit. But that Loki energy takes over. "I was looking at the wrong woman that night anyway. You did me a favor."

She drops her brows, looking skeptical. "What do you mean?"

"You're everything a man could ever want in a woman. You're beautiful. I have to force myself to look away from you when we're stretching, and I only do it because I don't want your dad to stab me to death with a skate blade."

She laughs softly. "You don't have to say that."

"I'm not just saying it. When you touch my ankle to stretch me, I get ... you know."

Hard. It makes me hard every time and I feel like a high school kid who can't control himself.

She waves a hand dismissively. "Men are like that. Melina probably gets it all the time."

"No, I've never gotten aroused from a female doctor or trainer touching me. Until you."

She holds my gaze for a moment and then looks down at her lap. "If you're willing to go to Hawaii with me, I'd really appreciate it."

Relief floods through me. I didn't like the idea of another man going with her. I don't even like the idea of my teammates getting stretching or other treatments from her.

"I'm all in." I start my car. "Let's make him regret every choice he's ever made."

She hums with amusement. "I don't know about that. Wait 'til you see my sister."

"Okay, new rule." I give her a serious look. "From now on, anytime I hear you put yourself down, you have to listen to three compliments and you can't argue about any of them." I don't wait for her to agree to the rule. "You have a very sexy voice. When we're stretching and you tell me to go as far as I can, I'm not thinking about stretching."

Her cheeks flush and her brows arch with surprise.

"Number two: I would crawl on my hands and knees for miles just to touch your breasts. Happily, they're incredible. And also, I think about the way you called me out on that bullshit pickup line every goddamn night. The compliment there is that I know there's nothing easy about you, and it's sexy as hell. Make me work for you, Talia. I will. I want to."

Her lips are parted slightly as she holds my gaze, her hazel eyes glossy with unshed tears. I didn't realize I felt all this for her until I said it. I like being around her, and not just because I'm attracted to her. She's funny and sharp, and I want to be more than friends with her, but the friends part is important, too.

I want to go buy whipped cream with her. Watch shows with her. Eat lunch with her.

And more. A lot more. But she's been hurt, and I have to move slow.

"I don't have the right words," she says, looking away. "Just ... thank you."

Her voice catches on the last part, and I put my car in drive, sensing that the conversation has gone as deep as she can handle right now.

Macintire did a number on her confidence. It's not a surprise to me that he didn't see what an amazing woman he had in her. If he doesn't regret it now, I'll make sure he does later.

# CHAPTER NINE

Talia

"Isaac's down!"

I'm not sure who's yelling from the bathroom in the locker room—it's a player, but not one I talk to often. Melina and I are sanitizing equipment in her room, and she immediately sets down the bottle of sanitizer in her hand.

"It's probably his vasovagal syncope," she says, rushing for the doorway. "Come on."

I set down the towel I'm holding, following. The guys are showering after practice, and I don't really want to go in the bathroom, but I follow Melina in.

Carter is outside one of the stalls, down on one knee.

"Don't," he's saying. "Let Melina check you over."

They are in the white-tiled space, which is thick with humidity from the showers. Lucien stands next to me as Carter talks to Melina.

"He'll be okay," he says. "This happens a lot."

I glance at him, my gaze locking onto the defined muscles of his chest, which has a light coating of dark hair. Kyle always had his chest waxed; I like that Lucien's has hair.

"Thirsty?" he asks, smirking.

I roll my eyes, ignoring the question. "Did he lose consciousness?"

"Probably, but just for a little bit. That's why he falls off the throne. Wasn't wearing his helmet either."

I gape at him. "His helmet?"

Lucien nods. "We got him a helmet to wear when he shits. The crap cap. He blows it off, though."

"Keep his head and neck as still as you can," Melina says.

Carter pulls Isaac from the stall, his hands hooked under Isaac's armpits.

"I'm fine," Isaac is griping. "Show's over, fuckers. Ouch! Fuck."

"Shut your piehole, Isaac!" Melina snaps. "How many times have I tried to get you to use a fiber supplement?"

Isaac's pants are around his ankles and even though I didn't mean to, I got a one-second glance at his midsection, and his penis is absurdly large—like the size of my forearm.

"I'm fine! Get your goddamn hands off me, Stanton!"

Carter ignores him, dragging Isaac across the floor and setting him down. Melina is trying to hold his head in a stable position. Bash brings a towel for Melina to put beneath his head and the floor.

"Does anything hurt?" she asks, kneeling beside him.

"I'm f—ah!" He cringes. "My neck."

Lucien blows out a breath next to me. Quiet settles over the room. The team has turned their losing streak around, everything going so well that they've all stopped shaving their faces out of super- stition. As their starting goalie, Isaac is a huge part of that.

"Call Caroline," Melina tells Carter. "And get Coach Turner."

"No!" Isaac barks. "Just give me a fucking minute, I'm fine."

"It's his neck," someone murmurs behind me.

Lucien is tense beside me. There's a palpable sense of dread in the whole bathroom about Isaac's condition.

"I'll get a C-collar," I say.

News of Isaac's fall has already spread around the locker room. The team had just finished practice, and many of us were planning to go out for lunch. The mood was light.

Now it's almost silent.

I find a cervical collar in the training supply closet. By the time I get back to the bathroom, my dad is kneeling beside Isaac, too.

"Be still and listen to her," Dad tells Isaac, his tone stern. "Melina and Caroline will tell you when you can move. I better not see you even blink until they tell you to."

"Without moving anything else, can you wiggle your toes for me?" Melina asks him.

Isaac complies, wiggling the toes on both his feet.

"Okay, good." She looks up at me. "Talia, will you grab a backboard and a blanket?"

I go grab what we need, and when I get back, the room has been cleared of everyone but Isaac, Carter, Lucien, Dad and Melina. A towel has been placed over Isaac's midsection. I set the board, which will keep his back immobile until Caroline can examine him, next to him.

She instructs Carter and Lucien on how to help her lift him onto the board. I did internships with two minor men's league hockey teams and a women's college track team, and I learned that it's important to not just treat a patient's body, but also to keep them from panicking.

Isaac's teammates are doing a good job with that.

"We've got you, man," Lucien says. "Just breathe."

"I think I'm okay." Isaac isn't agitated anymore. "But I get it, and I'll stay still until Caroline gets here."

They lift him onto the board, Lucien's defined biceps flexing with the movement. I'm probably a bad person for admiring his body at a time like this, but at least I'll be a happy woman while I burn in hell.

"Does anything hurt?" Melina asks him.

"Just my pride."

"Shit, man, we're all used to it," Carter says. "That's why we got you the seat belt and crap cap."

I move out of their way and stand next to my dad, who's off to the side with his arms crossed.

"I thought that seat belt and helmet were ridiculous, but I guess not," he says.

"How does he seat belt himself on a toilet?" I ask.

He runs a hand over his short salt and pepper hair, scoffing. "You should see the damn thing. He has to put the big loop around his chest and it attaches to the back of the wall in one of the stalls. So if he passes out, the loop keeps him upright. It's kind of ingenious."

"He needs a padded toilet stall," I say softly. "And yeah, a fiber supplement. Like Melina said."

Straining on the toilet can cause vasovagal syncope in some people. It starts with lightheadedness and can lead to passing out. I learned about it in school, but I've never seen an actual case.

"We'll see what the doc says," Dad says.

Melina leads the way out of the bathroom, Lucien and Carter carrying the board Isaac is now strapped to.

"I hate oatmeal!" Isaac is griping. "It's mushy."

"You don't have to like it," she counters. "Don't tell me you've never eaten something gross. I've seen the women you date."

I smile at Dad. "Hey, can I run something by you real quick? In your office?"

"Sure. I need to talk to Bruce for a minute. Meet me there in five."

———

DAD'S OFFICE is more inviting than his home. The walls of his four-bedroom home have impersonal art chosen by an interior designer, every room looking like it belongs in Architectural Digest.

Here, though, you can see him everywhere. There are photos of him on the walls spanning nearly the last three decades. He's grinning with teammates in some of the pictures, including one with Walter Denton, his former best friend and teammate, who died in a car crash a few years ago. A recreational golfer, he's shown posing with celebrities at golf tournaments and with pro golfers he's become friends with.

A bookcase is lined with personal photos, his second wife Angie scrubbed from the collection after their recent divorce. She deserves it after what she did to him. He was the last to know about her and their contractor.

Dad has his arms around my stepbrother, Chase, and my stepsister, Chloe, in one of the photos of them on a ski trip. I've always gotten along well with both of them, but I don't see them much anymore. Chase is a senior and Chloe is a freshman in college now.

In an older photo, Dad's down on one knee at Disney World, a six-year-old me grinning on one side of him and Audra, who was four at the time, on his other side.

I smile as I remember that trip. He'd married Angie, and we were spending a month of our summer with them. Dad went out of his way to make sure Audra and I felt included, and the trip to Disney World was just him and us. He must have paid a bundle for the white-glove service we got, bypassing all the lines.

Audra got an ice cream cone with three scoops of ice cream covered with rainbow sprinkles on that trip, and before she'd even tasted it, her ice cream plopped onto the ground.

I shared mine with her. We used to be so close. Anyone who messed with one of us was messing with both of us, and Dad taught us how to stand up for ourselves.

I never imagined my sister would be the one to hurt me like no one ever has. It was Kyle who confessed their affair to me, and all I could think of as he told me about it was that Audra would never do that to me.

Not only did she do it, but they were hooking up in the apartment I shared with Kyle at the time. In our bed.

I hid away part of myself on the day Kyle told me. It was just too painful to feel it all. He told me they were in love and that he was sorry. Audra said they didn't mean for it to happen.

Instead of the words sinking into me, I let them move past. I numbed myself with food and solitude. When my dad came to San Francisco in person to visit two months later, it was to break the news that they'd announced their engagement.

I cried for hours that night, Dad just quietly sitting on my couch with me. He's the only one who's seen me at my lowest. Mom sent both Audra and me an email telling us she loves us both and wouldn't be taking a side in our "situation".

Dad understood, though. My mom pulled the rug out from under his life with her affair, and then Angie did the same damn thing.

"Sorry, that took longer than expected," he says as he walks into the office. "What's up?"

I take in a deep breath and release it. "It's about the wedding."

He sits down behind his desk, waiting for me to continue. I remain standing because sitting across from him when he's at his desk makes me feel like I'm in the principal's office.

"I decided to go," I say.

He nods, not reacting.

"And Lucien is going to be my date."

His brows drop. "Lucien Beaumont."

I smile. "That's the one. How many Luciens do you know?"

"No."

"No what?"

He shakes his head. "Not Lucien. He knew goddamn well he wasn't allowed to touch you, and—"

"Dad, he hasn't."

"Talia, spending three days in Hawaii with your mother and Kyle motherfucking Macintire is going to be hard enough. I don't need to be worrying about

Beaumont taking advantage of you. You and I will go together."

When he looks at me, he still sees a fifteen-year-old girl. Maybe he always will.

"You don't need to worry about that, Dad."

He stands up, eyes wide. "He already did, didn't he? He's fucking dead."

I race over to the closed office door, pressing my back to it. Dad's face is red now, fury written in every line.

"Stop it! It's none of your business, but no, Lucien hasn't done anything with me, Dad."

He looks me square in the eye, trying to read me. "I know you better than that. I've seen the two of you talking during those stretching sessions. I'm going to stretch his nut sac off his fucking body. Get out of my way."

He's practically snarling. I can't let him get out of this room like this.

"I'm twenty-five, Dad. Twenty. Five. You're acting ridiculous."

"Because I know him. What are you doing getting involved with another hockey player?"

"We're not involved. He's become a friend. A friend. Nothing more."

Dad considers that for a few seconds, narrowing his eyes. "I know how it works. He's paving the way."

"I'm terrified of going to this wedding, Dad." My voice wavers with emotion. "It keeps me up at night."

His expression sobers.

"Not only have I gained weight, but everyone will be looking at me and talking behind my back." I take a deep breath, resolving not to cry. "My friend is coming with me for moral support. And that's the end of it. You know how hard this is going to be for me, so don't make it even harder."

He exhales heavily, looks at the ceiling, and turns away. "Fine. I'll switch my room to a double and he can take the couch."

"Every time you say something that makes me sound like a child, I'm going to tell you something about me you really don't want to know."

His brows shoot up. "Excuse me?"

I put up a palm. "I'm done, okay? He'll stay with me in the room you've kindly already booked for me."

He barks out a single note of laughter. "You think I'm paying for the room Beaumont's going to seduce my own daughter in?"

"I did a threesome once. And I was the only woman."

"No!" he yells, his expression a mixture of horrified and furious. "I can't unhear those words, Talia!"

"Then let's end this conversation. I'll see you at home later."

I walk out of his office then, his assistant Josh pretending to be immersed in whatever's on his computer screen. Then I wait around the corner, making sure Dad doesn't come flying out of his office to hunt down Lucien.

After about a minute, I decide it's safe for me to go.

Hopefully.

# CHAPTER TEN

Lucien

Isaac's out for at least a week with a cervical strain. Tonight was our first home game without him, and the mood in the locker room is somber.

We lost 4–3, but it doesn't matter that the game was close. Our backup goalie, Lennox, did his best, and I think he feels worse than any of us, which is saying something.

He's a twenty-one-year-old who moved up through the minors, and he's a hard worker. He puts in extra ice time before and after practice. This was a chance for him to prove himself, and from his expression, I know he's gutted he didn't do it.

"Hey, man." I hold my fist out to him. "Good

game. We fought hard. Best thing to do is let it go so you can be a hundred percent tomorrow."

He halfheartedly hits my fist with his own, his shoulders slumped.

Silas claps him on the shoulder as he passes. No one needs good teammates more than they do on the days they play like shit. Sometimes there's a reason—stress at home, the inevitable aches and pains of playing a grinding schedule—but sometimes you just don't have it and there's no explanation. Those games are the worst.

I used to lie awake half the night after a bad game, replaying every mistake and asking myself why I didn't do better. Our owner hired a mindset coach who works with us now, and it's been good for me.

A shitty mindset is like an injury. The body and mind are connected, and if your mind's not where it needs to be, your body won't be either.

Carter comes over to us, sweat dripping from his hair. He's stripped off everything but his pants and is about to get in the shower.

"Let's go get a drink at Duck's," he says, looking at me and then at Lennox.

"Yeah," I say.

Lennox just looks at the floor.

"Lennox?" Carter prods. "You in?"

He shakes his head. "I can't, man. Gotta watch film."

"I'm pulling rank on this one. You're in. The film can wait."

He walks away, the conversation over. Then he calls over his shoulder, "Tell everyone else, Lennox!"

Lennox grimaces, clearly aggravated. No one wants to be the guy who played a shit game and then tells everyone he's going out for drinks after.

"I'll do it, man," I tell him.

Talia is waiting for me in the training room, wearing sweatpants and a baggy Crush T-shirt. Her hair is piled on top of her head in a bun.

"Ready?" she asks.

I take a few more steps until I'm close enough that she's forced to crane her neck to keep her eyes on mine. I don't want anyone overhearing our conversation.

"Almost. Where are your usual pants?"

She furrows her brow, confused. "I didn't know I had usual pants."

"Yeah. Tight ones. So I can admire your ass in the mirror."

She flushes. "Please. I'm built like a Pixar Mom."

"Then I've got a thing for your Pixar Mom ass, and now I'll be laying three compliments on you."

She looks away like she's annoyed, but I don't miss the smile playing on her lips.

"I heard about the card you sent to Isaac. I like how you fit in so well here, and you're perceptive about what people need and when."

When her eyes find mine again, she's smiling for real. A full, radiant, no-sarcasm smile.

"Thank you. I really appreciate that."

I grin. "Look at you, getting better at taking compliments."

Her smile widens.

"Next," I say. "You have a beautiful smile. When I make you smile, it makes my whole day."

"Christ, get a room, you two," Bash mutters as he walks past.

I immediately take a step back. I didn't realize I was being so obvious, and if Turner knows how I feel about Talia, she'll never set foot in this locker room again.

"You're amazing at stretching me," I say, keeping my tone low. "My personal trainer measures my range of motion, and it's gotten better since I started working with you."

"Really?"

I nod. "I figured I was maxed out on range of motion, and he did, too."

"Can I see the numbers sometime?"

"Anytime. I keep them in my pants." I gesture at my crotch and she laughs.

She lets out a real, unguarded laugh, throwing

her head back. It's a bright, infectious sound I love bringing out of her.

Then she turns serious. "Okay, hip flexors. We have to get going. I heard you're going out with the guys."

"We both are."

She furrows her brow, still smiling. "We'll see about that."

I mimic her kneeling lunge position, stretching the muscles I used skating in the game. Leo joins us and does the stretch, too, not saying a word.

This has become our postgame routine. Talia helps Melina prep ice tubs and massage players who need it, and then Melina continues that work while Talia stretches anyone who wants to be led in stretches.

Melina's been pushing to get an assistant for a while now, and Talia's presence has demonstrated the need for it.

"Butterfly stretch," Talia says, putting her knees out and putting the soles of her feet together. "Just hold this and let it stretch your hips out."

She smiles at something behind me and I glance over my shoulder. Bash and Lennox have joined the group. I've been telling everyone how much stretching with her is helping me, and my teammates are finally getting the message.

The more guys who come to these sessions, the

higher the chances she can start to get paid for her work with a permanent place on our staff.

————

"I ACTUALLY MISS FART YOGA." Melina laughs. "No one tell Isaac. It's not that I miss the farts, I just miss how happy it makes him."

We're at the bar we go to after games, everyone sitting in a room off the main area that the owner keeps reserved for us after home games.

The whole team came, and so did Melina and a couple of our interns. Well, the whole team except Maxim. His wife is a ball and chain who doesn't let him go out.

"What can I get you?" our server asks.

"Start us out with ten orders of cheeseballs, ten potato skins, and ten mozzarella sticks," I say. "Put those on my tab."

When Bash told us this bar, which is only a couple of miles from our arena, was possibly closing because business wasn't good, we made it our official postgame hangout spot. The owner has since decorated the bar with Crush jerseys and memorabilia we supplied, and he plays every one of our games on the bar's televisions.

He wanted to change the bar's name to "Crushed", but of course, our team attorneys ruined it for bullshit legal reasons. So it's still called The Lucky Duck.

"Guess you're hungry," Talia quips after we order drinks.

"We take turns getting apps for everyone."

"Are you tired? You played twenty-seven minutes."

I shake my head. "That's about my usual."

"How's your left shoulder?"

I furrow my brow, amused. She was paying very close attention to me tonight. I got boarded hard in the second period and my shoulder took the brunt of the impact.

"It's good."

"Are you sure?"

"Yep, I'll rest it in Hawaii. What should I pack other than my Speedo?"

She considers. "I think ... that should cover it. Maybe some sunglasses?"

"I'd fucking love to show up at Macintire's wedding in a Speedo."

She rests her chin on her hand, her face turned toward me. "We've established why I have a voodoo doll collection of him, but what do you have against him?"

I bristle, remembering when that fucker was my teammate. "Too much to get into right now."

We're in a room with more than twenty people,

but I don't see anyone but her. I can't fucking wait for our trip. I booked us both in first class, even though Turner had already bought her a ticket, because I wanted to sit next to her on the flights.

Our drinks arrive, and she takes a sip of her unsweetened tea. I've noticed she doesn't drink alcohol when it's an option since the night we met. Though I usually get a beer when we come here, I'm having water. I didn't want her to be the only one not drinking alcohol.

"I want your thoughts on something," she says.

"Bikini."

"Bikini?" She furrows her brow. "Are we having the same conversation?"

"I figured you were going to ask if you should bring a bikini or a one-piece to Hawaii, and I was just weighing in."

She laughs. "That bikini would need some powerful straps to keep my girls contained."

"And is that a bad thing or a good thing?"

Biting her lip, she's quiet for a few seconds. Then she says, "This is a test, isn't it? I'm going to say it's a good thing."

It *was* a test to see if she was getting down on herself and needed to be hit with three compliments.

"Why is it a good thing?"

I've got a buzz, but it's entirely from her. I want

to grab her waist, pull her into my lap, and kiss her until she's breathless.

She leans in, whispering the answer to me. "Because I happen to have great boobs."

"I'll drink to that."

I pick up my red plastic cup and she grabs hers. We clink them together and both drink, alone in our own private bubble, despite the many people surrounding us.

# CHAPTER ELEVEN

Talia

"Maybe alcohol will help," Mara suggests. "It's gotten me through some rough times."

I sigh softly and sip my unsweet tea. "Trust me, I'd love to get so smashed I don't even know I'm on an airplane in the morning, but then I'll end up with the same crushing anxiety and a hangover, too."

"There's always meth." She sips her glass of wine. "Unless you want to keep your teeth?"

She has a way of making my worries feel a little lighter. I'd planned to meet up with her, Suki, and Lainey for drinks tonight, but Suki had to cancel because Charlotte is sick.

"I'm fairly attached to my teeth," I say lightly.

"Do you ever take gummies?" Lainey asks. "They really take the edge off."

"I have a stash. What dosage makes you forget you've made the worst decision of your life?"

Mara smiles. "I love that you're going. It's savage as fuck. What's something funny or embarrassing about your ex that only you know?"

"Let's see ... he gets hemorrhoids from sitting on the toilet too long. And he liked being spanked during sex. I don't know if he still does."

Mara and Lainey get a good laugh out of that tidbit.

"Elaborate on the spanking," Mara says.

"When he was drunk, it took five business days for him to come during sex. It was crazy. So when I couldn't stand the thrusting and grunting any more, I'd spank his ass and call him a naughty boy and he'd immediately get off."

Mara points at me, her eyes bright with amusement. "Every time you look at him on this trip, I want you to think about that. You're being saved from a lifetime of spanking a narcissistic man-child."

Lainey glances at her watch. "Sorry, guys. I have to go. We decided at the last minute to go to Columbus for a few days, and Bash wants to drive there tonight." She stands up and gets her coat, which is hanging on the back of her chair. "Don't leave us hanging, Talia. Keep us updated in the group text."

I stand up and hug her. "Have a great break with your husband. Thanks for being such a good friend to me."

"Right back at you. Have fun with Lucien. You'll be in Hawaii, how can you not have fun?"

Worry gnaws at my stomach. Why am I doing this to myself? I let my pride make this decision, and the chances of that choice backfiring are very high.

"At least I'll get lei'd," I say weakly. "Spelled l-e-i, of course."

Mara gives me a pointed look. "Sweetie, if you don't know you and Lucien are going to hook up on this trip, you're the only one."

My stomach does another full roll of nervousness. Or maybe it's excitement? Either way, I do have enough sense left to not dig myself into an even deeper hole.

"Lucien and I are just friends."

Mara purses her lips and meets Lainey's gaze. "Isn't she adorable? We're going to be shopping for wedding dresses with her by this time next year."

"Strapless all the way," Lainey says. "She's going to be a beautiful bride."

"Stop!" My face heats as I take cash out of my wallet to leave on the table for my tea. "Men and women can be just friends, you know."

"Of course they can," Mara says. "But not you and Lucien. And I'm guessing you won't have to spank that one to get him off, girl."

"Lucien's a great guy," Lainey says. "Bash told me he's really close with his sister. When she had cancer, he stepped in and helped a lot."

My heartstrings don't just get tugged by learning that. It's more like a powerful yank. He's good to his sister, and that says a lot about his character.

No, I'm not going there. Lucien is a hockey player. I'll take his friendship and his compliments, but I will *not* get stupid over him. Fool me once and all.

"Speaking of Lucien, I'm supposed to meet up with him to go over our packing lists," I say, standing up.

"Don't forget condoms," Mara says, smirking. "Lots of condoms."

"And lube," Lainey adds.

My brows shoot up in surprise. "You look so sweet and innocent, and then you tell me to bring lube on a trip where no sex will be taking place."

She shrugs. "Lie to us all you want, just don't lie to yourself. Prep your lady bits and bring lube."

That fluttering sensation in my stomach returns. Probably just from the mention of having sex. It's been a long time. Kyle and I hadn't had sex in months when he broke things off.

"I just want to get through this," I say. "That's it. Just survive it without crying in front of Kyle or Audra. Lucien is my emotional support human. Nothing more."

———

LUCIEN'S HOUSE IS COZY. Even though the massive brick home is near the back of a gated community, almost an hour outside of Cleveland, it's a lot more comfortable than I expected.

The leather furniture has throw pillows and a chunky throw blanket draped over the back of the couch. A fire crackles in the fireplace, a giant painting of a little cabin with glowing light emanating from the windows during a snowstorm hangs over the mantle.

"Do you have a wife you haven't mentioned?" I ask as I shed my coat and look around the space.

"Nope. I picked most of this stuff out myself. My sister helped some." He picks up my coat. "I'll hang this up for you."

That's ... unexpected. Kyle was my first serious boyfriend and he threw his coat wherever when he came inside, then flopped onto his couch to play video games.

"Thanks. Is it just you and your sister? Any other siblings?"

"Just me and Calla. She actually got some great news a couple days ago. She's a breast cancer survivor. Her first follow-up scan was inconclusive, so she had to go back for more. It was really stressful, but she's all clear."

"I'm so glad to hear that."

He comes back into the large living room, which is open to the modern kitchen with white cabinetry and dark stone counters. "We lost our mom to breast cancer when we were both teenagers, so it was ..." He shakes his head. "I don't even know how to describe the way I felt when she told me."

"I can't imagine. I'm so sorry about your mom."

Warmth flickers in his eyes as he nods. "Anyway, Calla's good. Have you eaten? I saved you some lasagna."

I furrow my brow and follow him to the kitchen area. "I'm good, thanks. You cook, too?"

He turns to face me, folding his arms. His expression is amused. "What do you mean, too?"

I look around. "I wasn't expecting this."

"You thought I'd just have two recliners and a big-screen TV?"

"Kind of," I admit.

"Fully functioning adult here. I don't cook, though. There's a chef who preps meals for a bunch of us single guys on the team that we can freeze and eat when we're home."

I smile, my shoulders sinking with relief. "Okay, I feel a little bit better about living with my dad and surviving on grilled cheese sandwiches."

He opens the refrigerator and takes out a glass pitcher of what looks like unsweet tea. "Come on, try this lasagna. It's fantastic."

He dishes some of the cheesy, gooey pasta onto a plate and pours us both a glass of tea.

"So you wanted to run something by me when we were at Lucky's, but you never did."

I set my fork down, remembering what I wanted to ask him. "Right. So you know about my job working with physically and mentally disabled people. I was thinking ... what if I put together a thing where some of the guys on the team could play a game of wheelchair hockey against a team of wheelchair users who are also athletes? Maybe I could work with Special Olympics."

"It's a great idea. I can't think of any of the guys who wouldn't want to do it."

"Yeah?" I've been knocking around the idea for a while now, and I like that he's on board. "I thought it would be neat to spotlight what it's like to play hockey as a wheelchair user."

"We're probably gonna get smoked."

I laugh. "Longtime wheelchair users are really good at maneuvering them, so you might."

"Do you know Briana? She runs the Crush Foundation and I think she'll be able to help with whatever you need."

"I guess I should check with the front office first."

"Tell them the players want to do it." He gestures at my plate. "Now eat, and I'll grab my packing list."

"Thanks for being my emotional support human."

"Anytime."

The lasagna is so damn good. I was planning to only eat a couple of bites and then say I'm full, but screw that. It's delicious. And a nice thing about Lucien and me just being friends is that I don't have to pretend I like girl dinners. A few crackers and a piece of cheese are *not* dinner.

Lucien passes me his list and I read it over. He has neat, blocky handwriting.

"I just want to make sure you know I fucking hate Macintire," he says.

I look up from the paper. "I mean, same? Don't tell me he got with your sister, too."

He balks. "I wouldn't let that fucker within ten feet of Calla. Macintire didn't just fuck me over; he fucked over our entire team when we were teammates. He doesn't even deserve to be called anyone's teammate."

"What did he do?"

Lucien's gaze is on my lap, his lips quirking with

a smile when his eyes flick up to mine. "Nice to see you back in leggings. I'm gonna need a beer for this conversation."

He takes a bottled Guinness from his fridge and pops the top off with an opener, taking a long drink. Then he sets the bottle on the counter and leans back against it, crossing his arms.

"We had some concerns about our coach at the time. And when I say we, I mean the top five on the team. Macintire wasn't in that group, that's for goddamn sure. He's always been second or third string, and he resented our first offensive line. Thought he was better than them." He picks up the bottle and takes another drink. "So anyway, our captain decided we needed to bring the rest of the team in on the conversation about our coach. He was drinking a lot. Had alcohol on his breath at practices and games. We found him passed out in his office more than once. He wasn't doing his job, and the team was suffering for it. We had to decide whether we were going to have an intervention and try to force him into rehab, or talk to the GM."

"Max Gregory," I say softly.

Anyone who follows hockey knows what happened to Max Gregory. It was a tragedy.

Lucien nods grimly. "It was a tough situation. We cared about him, of course, but also, our team was playing like shit because our coach was checked out. There was a group text that was for players only, and we discussed it there. Macintire leaked the texts to a reporter."

My jaw drops. "It was him? I remember when that happened."

"It ended Hartford's career. No coach would touch him. And it fucked a lot of other guys over, too."

I'm stunned. But now that I think about it …

"Kyle moved up to the first line when Gregory quit."

Lucien nods. "That's why he did it. Looking out for number one, like always. And Gregory died of alcohol poisoning within a week of quitting. He didn't deserve that—to have his shit blasted all over the internet, and to know—" He looks away. "It's hard for me to talk about it. All of us feel partially responsible for Gregory's death."

I can't stop myself from walking over and hugging him. He's rock solid, and he smells amazing, his cologne carrying notes of pine and cedar.

"I'm so sorry."

He holds me tightly. And when we finally pull apart a few seconds later, I'm not terrified anymore.

"Thank you for coming with me. Fuck him, and fuck Audra. We're going to have a great time."

His hand is still on my hip. Friends touch each other's hips, right?

"Maybe we'll get to see some fireworks," he says.

I grin. "If not, we'll just have to start some."

# CHAPTER TWELVE

Lucien

"Talia. We're so glad you're here."

Audra says her sister's name with a note of pity, and I slide an arm around Talia's waist and pull her against me, saving her from Audra's hug.

"You must be Audra. I'm Lucien Beaumont, nice to meet you."

Audra's expression brightens as she shakes my hand. "I had no idea Talia was seeing someone! And a hockey player!" She shoots Coach Turner a mock look of surprise. "I can't believe you're okay with this, Dad."

"Beaumont's a great guy," Coach says.

Audra met us as soon as we arrived at the front

entrance to the resort everyone is staying at for the wedding. We're on the Big Island, where Audra and Kyle's beach ceremony is planned for the day after tomorrow.

A bellhop arrives to take our bags and we follow Audra into the resort's lobby.

She's a little taller and not as pretty as Talia. Talia has sexy curves and expressive eyes, but her sister is forgettable.

A concierge greets us and offers to handle our check-in. Coach Turner and I both reach for our wallets, and he shoots me a glare.

"I'm paying for both rooms," he says.

"I appreciate that, Coach, but I've got ours."

He hates that I'm sharing a room with Talia. I don't need to hear him say it to know it.

"Fine," he says smoothly, passing the concierge his card.

"So, Talia," Audra says. "I have an extra bridesmaid dress in case you change your mind. It might need to be altered, because I didn't realize your body had changed so much, but I'll find someone to do it if you want. I'd love to have you in the bridal party."

What a bitch. I fight my urge to tell Audra to fuck off, but Talia can stand up for herself.

"That's okay," Talia says lightly.

"My other daughter has arrived!"

A tall, thin woman with a light-blond bob and a

deep tan is approaching us, her arms wide open. Coach Turner sighs heavily.

"Hi, Mom," Talia says with absolutely zero enthusiasm.

They hug, her mom stepping back after doing a once-over of her daughter, then smiling tightly and saying, "Let's do some shopping while you're here. I'll get you some clothes cut for your figure."

"Her clothes are just fine," Coach Turner says.

"Mom, this is Lucien Beaumont," Talia says.

I take her hand and extend my other one to her mother. Her expression softens and she leans in for a half hug.

"Lucien. I'm so glad Talia is seeing someone. I'm Renee Carlisle."

"Well, we're going to get settled in our rooms," Coach Turner says.

Audra takes a step closer to Talia. "Can we talk alone?"

"Oh, I need to take a shower and change. The schedule says we have a thing in like an hour and a half."

"It won't take long."

I lie without even thinking about it. "My neck is stiff from the flight. Talia has magic hands; she's going to work on it for me."

"Right," Talia agrees. "We'll see you for the dinner thing."

"It's a sunset cruise." Audra's tone is corrective, like she's offended that Talia didn't call it the right thing.

I put a hand on Talia's lower back as we walk away.

"I hate this already," she says softly. "Why did I come?"

"I promise you'll have fun." I press the up button on the elevator. "Just trust me."

———

THE HAWAIIAN SUNSET paints the sky in dramatic streaks of pink and orange, but I'm too distracted by Talia to enjoy it. Her red dress accentuates her curves and shows off her spectacular legs. She's got heels and a little black sweater on, her gaze finding mine as she talks to one of the bridesmaids.

"You mind, Coach?" I gesture at the seat next to him, part of a built-in bench with a padded seat cover.

"Go ahead."

He's holding a glass of whiskey, and I can tell from his closed-off expression that he's not enjoying the sunset cruise.

"Not a fan of food on toothpicks?" I ask.

"I'm not a fan of Kyle Macintire. But you know that already."

He's in a bad position. Talia's told me her dad has been supportive of her since the breakup, and he asked her if she was okay with him going to the wedding.

"We have that in common, Coach."

He gives me a wry smile. "On this trip, call me Noel."

I don't think I could get his first name out of my mouth unless someone had a gun to my head. He's my coach, and he always will be. Even if I play for a different team or retire, I'll always call him Coach to his face, and either Coach or Turner when I'm talking to someone else about him.

"Did you bring any work with you?" I ask.

"Always."

The large sailboat we're on is crowded with not just the huge bridal party, but lots of other family members and guests that Audra and Kyle invited. Kyle's mom cried when she saw Talia, embracing her warmly and telling her how much she missed her.

"So you two are a thing now?" Coach asks me, his tone bristly.

I shrug a shoulder. "We would be if she wanted to be."

He pinches his brows together. "Then what's with telling everyone you are? And all the touching?"

He can be the nicest guy in the world, or the grouchiest bastard. I know he just wants to protect his daughter, though. I tip my beer bottle to my mouth, speaking in a low tone right before I take a drink, so my mouth is covered.

"Because she feels more confident with people thinking she's moved on."

His scowl falls away. "But she hasn't?"

"You'd have to ask her. I think she has, but being here is still tough for her."

He exhales heavily. "Thanks for being here for her. I thought it would be enough if I was here, but ... thanks."

"I want to be here. Talia's awesome."

Kyle's been avoiding me. He only greeted Talia when she was pulled aside to meet someone. I catch sight of him holding on to the side of the sailboat, puking his guts out.

"Looks like Kyle is sick. Shame."

Coach scoffs. "Hope he chokes on it."

"You doing the paddleboarding group thing tomorrow?"

He groans. "I don't know."

"I guess there's a volcano hike, too. In the afternoon."

Coach shakes his head, draining the last of the whiskey from his glass. "Beaumont, I'd rather walk into a live volcano than spend time with my ex-wife."

"Hang out with me and Talia, then."

He clears his throat. "I'll be frank. Watching you hit on my daughter is also not fun."

I smile, but stop myself from laughing. "That's fair. Just wanted you to know you've got people here."

"Thanks. I agreed to do this and the ceremony. That's it."

Coach has been in a darker mood since his recent divorce. Which I get, because her cheating and leaving him for their contractor was an ugly, public thing. His ex, Angie, accused him of being emotionally unavailable and married to his work.

Talia comes over to us, saving me from trying to make more small talk with Turner. She's radiant, her natural waves pinned up with a few pieces loose around her face.

"Lucien, this is my cousin Kimmie. Kimmie, Lucien Beaumont."

Kimmie looks around thirty. She's got wild dark curls and her eyes remind me of Talia's.

"Lucien, I'm so happy to meet you." She leans in to hug me.

"Great to meet you, too, Kimmie."

She beams at Talia. "Girl, you totally traded up. He is delicious."

Coach mutters something under his breath. I stand up so I'm beside Talia. She takes my hand.

"He's pretty great," she agrees.

There's a commotion on the other end of the boat, and we all turn to look.

"No, sir," one of the boat's crew members says to Kyle.

Kyle shakes his head, looking disgusted. Audra is trying to lead him somewhere, and he's not happy about it.

Kimmie turns to us and says, "They're telling him not to vomit over the side of the boat. He got some on the boat and the captain is not happy."

When Kyle glances at our group, his gaze stops on me. He squints and I can read his lips as he says, "What the hell is he doing here?"

He looks pissed. I knew he would be. I keep my expression neutral. Talia gently squeezes my hand.

"Here we go," she says softly as Kyle shakes off Audra's arm and stomps over to us.

Coach Turner gets up and stands on my other side, leaning over to speak in my ear.

"If he starts something, you finish it."

"I will."

Kyle stumbles and comes to a stop, swallowing. I hope he's swallowing his own puke. After a couple seconds, he resumes his trek over to us.

"What the hell is he doing here?" He fires the question at Talia.

"He's my date. Didn't Audra tell you?"

Kyle looks over his shoulder at Audra, whose expression is horrified.

"Kyle, what are you doing?" she whisper-hisses. "Everyone's looking."

"You did this on purpose," he says to me, seething.

It's Coach Turner who steps in.

"Kyle, Lucien is on my team. It's how he and Talia met. If you have a problem with him being here, you can address it with me. Privately."

"Yes." Audra puts both hands on his shoulders, trying to move him away from us. "Privately." She lets out a loud, fake laugh. "You hockey players. Always fighting!"

Kyle's resisting Audra's efforts to move him, looking between me and his future father-in-law. He wants to rush me so fucking badly. Other than games, we haven't seen each other since right after he threw me and the rest of our team under the bus. Everything imploded after that. I got traded.

I let go of Talia's hand and put my arm around her instead, stroking my thumb over her bare shoulder. Macintire's expression darkens. Talia leans against me, and just when I think Macintire's going to say fuck it and throw a punch, he does something else instead.

He bends down and pukes again, orange vomit landing on Audra's strappy little shoes and perfectly manicured feet. There's a collective gasp, someone pulling out a camera phone to take a photo.

"Sorry, babe," Kyle says weakly. "I couldn't help it."

Audra is about to blow. Her face is red and she keeps opening her mouth and closing it again. She looks like a fish lying on a shoreline.

"Ma'am, let us help you with this," one of the boat's crew members says.

Someone brings a mop and a woman—I think it's Audra's maid of honor—shoots Talia a dirty look before leading Audra away by the arm.

Kyle gets to his feet and walks away, not looking back at us.

Talia's eyes meet mine, a wicked gleam swirling in with the green and brown shades. "Okay. I should've believed you when you said we'd have a great time."

# CHAPTER THIRTEEN

Talia

I POUR myself a cup of the coffee Lucien brewed in our room, burning my mouth on the first sip.

I'm exhausted after a long, mostly sleepless night. I slept on the flight here and Lucien didn't, so when we went to bed last night, he fell asleep fast.

Not me. I just lay there, either looking at him or thinking about him. The king-size bed is big enough that we weren't touching, but I was aware of him every second. His warmth. His closeness. His bare chest and arms. The dark locks of hair falling over his forehead.

Lucien isn't what he's supposed to be. He's supposed to look right past me because I have a thick waist. Or want me, but only for sex. I spent all those months alone on my couch with snacks and comfort shows, figuring things out. And I realized that men in general—and hockey players in particular—are transactional. They're careful with the energy they spend on a woman.

Then Lucien blew my realizations to shreds. He came with me on this trip, which is taking up his entire five-day break from hockey. And while I know from his compliments and flirting that he's interested in me, I've never felt pressured. He's never shown agitation or impatience.

It's confusing as hell. Everything was easier when I expected all men to disappoint me.

He opens the bathroom door and steam escapes the room as he walks out and says, "Hey, good morning."

"Morning. Thanks for the coffee."

He's only wearing a towel around his waist, and even though I've seen him this way many times in the locker room, it's another thing entirely to be alone in a hotel room with him. If he dropped the towel, I could see every inch of him.

His dark, wavy hair is wet and messy. The closer he gets to me, the dizzier I feel. His woodsy, masculine scent is like a drug I can't get enough of.

"I've got a plan for today." He stops just a couple

feet away from me, so close I can see the wetness of his dark, thick eyelashes.

I drink the too-hot coffee, trying to distract myself from his presence. If he looks at my nipples, it's over. He'll see how turned on I am.

"What is it?" My voice is a croak, my mouth protesting the scalding coffee.

"We're going to lay it on thick. Lots of affection and laughing. They'll think we're the happiest couple in the fucking world."

I'll never forget the way I felt last night when Kyle stormed over to us in a rage. He looked between me and Lucien like we'd betrayed him. Like I was supposed to be the scorned, sad ex who couldn't stop crying.

Kyle never laid a hand on me, but he would punch things when he was really angry, and it scared me. There was no fear with Lucien beside me, though. Between him and my Dad, Kyle wouldn't even make it to me before he found himself tossed overboard.

"I'm going to be awkward," I admit. "I've never been in a relationship with much affection."

He scoffs. "Yeah, that tracks, knowing Macintire."

I back up, both to lower my blood pressure and to make sure he can't smell my morning breath, now laced with coffee. "Should I just pet your head like you're a dog?"

He smiles, his eyes warm. "You're pretty killer at dry delivery, Turner."

Damn. Every compliment from him is like a shot of endorphins injected directly into my veins.

"When you scratch my ears, I should thump my leg, right?"

"Just follow my lead. I'll tell you what to do."

A laugh bursts out of me. "Is this going to involve blow jobs?"

"No, but there will be kissing."

My heart skips about ten beats, but I try to look unbothered. "Okay."

He walks over to me, his closeness making my stomach flutter with awareness. He wasn't supposed to do this, either. I'd resolved to be uncharmable. No man would make me weak in the knees ever again. But my knees aren't exactly steady right now.

"Okay, this is the move," he says softly. "When I do this, I'm about to kiss you."

He curls his index finger, using his knuckle to tilt my chin up. He looks into my eyes, leaning closer.

"No!" I step back. "Not yet, I haven't brushed my teeth."

He rolls his eyes and grins. "Go do it then, so we can practice."

"You think I need to practice kissing?"

His playful grin makes me forget I don't want to let myself fall for him. "Definitely. We both do."

I go into the still-steamy bathroom and wipe my palm over the mirror so I can see myself. My hair is everywhere. I look like hell, and Lucien still wants to kiss me.

I'm thorough with the teeth brushing, and I pull my hair up into a messy bun and wash my face, too. The steam fog is clearing from the bathroom mirror, and I smile at my reflection.

This trip wasn't supposed to be fun. It was supposed to be horrible. Once again, Lucien is turning my expectations upside down.

I take a deep breath and open the bathroom door. He's right there, and he cups my cheek with his hand and puts the other hand on the small of my back, pulling us together.

A squeak of surprise comes out of me as his mouth covers mine. I melt into him then, putting my arms around his neck. His warm, sensual kiss awakens not just my mouth, but my entire body. I feel it all the way down to the tips of my toes.

I've never been kissed like this. I slide a hand up into his hair, plowing my fingers over his scalp. He groans in response and pulls me tighter against him, his tongue brushing over mine.

I don't want to pull away from him. Not ever. But my body makes me—so I can breathe in air. He doesn't release his hold on me. Both his arms are around my waist now, and he's bending down, his forehead resting lightly against mine.

"That's my other move," he says against my lips.

"It's good." I'm still breathless. "I can see how that one works well for you."

"No squealing like you're not used to it. Just kiss me back like I'm your man and you don't care who knows it. Like I kiss you this way eighteen times a day."

I don't put the back of my palm over my forehead like I'm about to pass out, but inside I. Am. Swooning. I'm swooning hard.

All I can do is nod. "Eighteen times a day. Got it."

He steps back and I immediately miss his heat and closeness. "Have you ever paddleboarded?"

"What?"

Paddleboarding. Our activities today are learning paddleboarding and hiking a volcano with the bridal party and the rest of the family members.

"Oh. Uh ... I did it once. I'm not good at it."

"I'm decent."

Of course he is. How can he be thinking about paddleboarding when I'm still reeling from that kiss? It was like that scene in *The Wizard of Oz* where everything switches from black and white to color.

That's how amazing a kiss can be. I can't unknow that now.

"You okay with me smacking your ass or not?"

I furrow my brow. "Right now?"

He quirks a brow, amused. "No, in general. Some guys smack their woman's ass."

"Not in public, no. I'll probably punch you if you smack my ass in public."

"Got it, only in private." He winks.

Today is either going to be amazing or a catastrophe. I honestly don't know which it'll be. But it definitely won't be boring with Lucien around.

———

"No lessons." The guy who was supposed to teach our group paddleboarding lessons points at the sign stuck in the sand. "Like I said, there's a box jellyfish advisory. All our lessons are canceled today."

"No!" Audra pouts. "I have the photographer coming and everything." She looks at Kyle, like he can do anything about it.

He's glaring at Lucien, who has his arm around me. I'm wearing a two-piece swimsuit, but it has a high waist and a long top, so only about an inch of my midriff shows. It's cut to maximize my breasts, though, which I think look spectacular. I have a wrap around my waist and a straw hat on my head.

"We'll find something else to do," one of the bridesmaids, Kayla, says. "Maybe kayaking?"

"We're not renting kayaks today, either," the

guide says. He looks at Kyle and Audra. "We'll issue a full refund for today. Enjoy the rest of your trip."

"Well, this sucks," Audra says glumly as the guide walks away. "I really wanted to paddleboard on this trip."

"Maybe we can do it the day after the wedding," Kayla says.

The bridesmaids are easily identifiable because they're all wearing cropped white T-shirts that say "Bridesmaid," with Audra and Kyle's names and wedding date. I snuck a photo of one of them earlier and sent it to Suki, Mara, and Lainey.

Lucien strips off his T-shirt and drops it to the sand. "I've always wondered what it feels like to get stung by a jellyfish."

One of Kyle's groomsmen lets out a single note of laughter. "It hurts like fuck, man. Don't do it."

Now I know why none of his groomsmen are hockey players. Lucien said it's well known that all of his former teammates from Vancouver hate him, and why. They all made sure no one else would get burned by trusting him like they did.

"I'm gonna go for a swim," Lucien says, kissing my temple.

I gape at him. "What? Why?"

He gestures to the vinegar rinsing station nearby. "I'll rinse off if I get stung."

He slides out of his flip-flops. Everyone is

looking at him like he's out of his mind, including me.

"I'll go too." Kyle pulls his T-shirt off.

I'm not surprised. His ego is too massive to stand here while Lucien swims with jellyfish.

"Want to race?" Lucien asks.

"Hell yeah. I'm not saving your ass if you drown."

Lucien points at a buoy in the water. "Around that and back?"

"Kyle, no," Audra says sharply. "You are not doing this. I don't want your face all stung up on our wedding day."

He sneers at her. "Keep your panties on. I'll be fine."

One of the bridesmaids I don't know, gasps, probably at his dismissive tone.

"What the fuck, man?" one of the groomsmen, Mark, says. "I guess I have to do it, too."

"No one has to do it!" Audra cries. "This is stupid!"

I agree with her, but I'm not going to undercut Lucien by saying that in front of everyone. He must have a reason for doing this.

"Three, two, one, go!" Lucien says.

He and Kyle run into the water and the wedding photographer walks up to us. At least I assume that's who it is. She has a huge camera around her neck and a bag over her shoulder.

Audra covers her face with her hands, crouching down. I'm quietly picturing Kyle's face being red and swollen in all their wedding photos, and I'm probably a bad person for how giddy it makes me.

They're halfway to the buoy when Kyle yells out, "Fuck!"

He keeps swimming, though. The two of them are side by side, both swimming hard and fast.

They make it around the buoy, Audra standing now and biting her lip as she watches.

Kyle falters about a third of the way back. Lucien moves like a machine, nothing slowing him down.

"He got stung," Kayla says softly.

When Lucien runs up onto the beach, he runs his hands over his hair, grinning. "A couple of 'em got me. It's not so bad, though."

Not so bad? He has several bright-red welts on his chest, and a couple more on one of his biceps.

"It doesn't hurt?" I approach him, concerned.

I've taken enough first aid classes to know that jellyfish stings hurt. It's like getting whipped with a red-hot whip.

"Nah."

Kyle gasps for breath as he reaches a point where he can stand, doubling over. Two of his groomsmen run out to help him.

"I got fucking nailed!" he yells, standing up and refusing their offers of help. "It fucking burns!"

"You idiot." Audra is seething.

Lucien picks up his T-shirt and puts it back on, unfazed. The groomsmen and bridesmaids are all fussing over Kyle, one of the groomsmen pulling his swim trunks down and yelling, "You want me to piss on it?"

Kyle's legs and back got stung. He's moaning and groaning dramatically, the photographer quietly snapping away.

"My work here is done," Lucien whispers. "Want to go grab breakfast?"

I spent so long getting ready, worried about what I was wearing, that we didn't have time to eat before we came.

"Sure."

We sneak away from the chaos, and he takes my hand. I'm still not sure what happened, but Lucien brought his Loki energy out at the perfect time.

"Want to find a restaurant nearby?" I ask him.

He nods, his expression grim. "After we find a rinsing station at another beach. These stings hurt like a motherfucker. I just didn't want to let on in front of them."

I never thought I'd be turned on by a man deliberately getting stung by jellyfish. But Lucien is full of surprises.

# CHAPTER FOURTEEN

Lucien

TALIA HOLDS out her phone to take a selfie of us with the jungle as a backdrop.

"Incoming," I whisper, turning to kiss her.

She takes two pictures of us kissing, then tucks her phone back into the canvas cross-body bag that rests on her hip.

"That energy drink is really helping," she says. "I could carry you the rest of the way to the top if you want me to."

I smile and shake my head. "Yeah, good luck with that."

It's been five hours since the jellyfish branding, and the pain is finally manageable. This morning, we went to a rinsing station, and it helped, but Talia had to go buy more vinegar and pour it on the stings in our hotel shower.

I stood there in my underwear, and it took all my self-control not to bitch and moan the entire time. I'm not sure even Loki would've gotten himself stung by jellyfish on purpose. I was showing off for Talia, and I'm only functional because of the prescription-strength pain reliever she had in her bag.

Now we're on a group hike with the bridal party, and the rest of them are doing a scavenger hunt. Talia and I just wanted to enjoy the scenery.

"So how did you two meet?" Audra's bridesmaid, Kayla, asks us from nearby.

I smile at the memory of Talia scowling at me in her Unabomber hoodie at the bar where we met.

"I was hitting on another woman and Talia shot me down."

Talia laughs at my description. "His pickup line was so cringe. He asked her if her name was Anesthesia."

Kayla groans.

"I didn't use that line, I said I had a friend who was going to use it."

Talia gives me a pointed look. "But you didn't. Which actually makes it worse."

I grin and take her hand. "Yet here we are. You can't get enough of me."

"Enjoying my leftovers, Beaumont?" Kyle calls out from ahead of us.

Hurt flickers across Talia's face and I release her hand. Kyle's around twenty feet in front of us, and he doesn't even know I'm coming when I slam into him from behind and we both land on the ground.

"What the hell?" Audra shouts.

I land a punch to his gut that makes him grunt. The pain from the jellyfish stings reignites, but I just keep punching. I roll so I can get on top of him and pound his face, more feral than I've ever been in any hockey fight. The punches he's getting in don't even register.

"Don't ever talk about her." I grab the collar of his shirt and pull him up from the ground. "If her name ever comes out of your mouth again, I'll break your fucking legs."

Something pummels into me, sending me flying. I'm buried beneath something heavy and I can't breathe.

It's not until Kyle's groomsman gets off me that I realize it was him. His name's Brad, and he weighs a solid two hundred and fifty pounds. Another groomsman is on the ground with Kyle, holding him back.

"Enough!" Audra yells, standing in the space between me and Kyle with her hands out.

She looks unhinged, a vein visible in her forehead. When she turns to face Talia, her expression is murderous.

"You brought him here to ruin our wedding, didn't you? You can't stand the idea that he's happier with me and that you were rejected."

I shove Brad's arm off and walk away, my blood boiling. If I wasn't the kind of man who'd never raise his hand to a woman, I'd be all over Talia's bitch of a sister.

"I don't care whether or not you two are happy," Talia says, shrugging. "I'm with Lucien now, and that's why I brought him."

Audra stomps over to Talia, pointing right in her face. Hands on my hips, I watch her every movement. If she touches Talia, we're going to have a problem.

"Everything's been a goddamn disaster since you two got here! I've been puked on and humiliated! My fiancé has jellyfish stings all over and he's going to have a black eye and a fat lip during our wedding ceremony!"

Talia raises her chin and fires back. "So you're saying we made Kyle seasick?"

Audra scowls and stomps her foot. "No, but the

jellyfish thing was him!" she points a finger with a long red nail at me. "And the fight!"

I put my hands in the air. "He knew damn well that was going to happen. Talking shit about Talia is a 'fuck around and find out' situation." I glance around at the shocked faces of the bridal party. "Anyone else got something to say?"

Kyle's on his feet now. He wipes the back of his hand beneath his bleeding nose and sneers at me.

"Fuck you, Beaumont." He spits on the ground. "You're all cheap shots and empty chirps. I'm ready to finish what you started."

"No!" Audra cries. "I don't want you standing at the altar in a fucking neck brace, Kyle! Your jacked-up face is already going to ruin enough."

Kyle's torn between coming for me and keeping his bride-to-be happy.

"Hey babe," I call, glancing at Talia. "You mind if I fight him?"

"Not at all." She smiles. "Your balls belong entirely to you."

Audra lets out a bloodcurdling scream that shuts everyone up.

"Stop! Ruining! My wedding!" She looks around at everyone, her eyes wild. "Tomorrow is *my day*, and I will personally dismember anyone who ruins it."

Talia and I exchange a quick look of concern.

"I think Lucien and I should go back home," she says softly.

"No!" Audra cries. "Every fucking member of my fucked-up fucking family is going to be in my wedding pictures! That includes you, Talia."

Talia's lips part with surprise. "I'm not going to be in your wedding photos. That's ridiculous, given my history with Kyle."

"You're still my sister." Audra's voice breaks with emotion.

Talia sighs softly. "Yes. And if you need a kidney or something like that, I'm in. But don't ask me to stand there and smile for your wedding pictures."

"I thought you'd moved on," Audra says smugly, crossing her arms.

"I have."

Her gaze flicks to me, and something in her eyes makes me walk over to stand beside her. I take her hand, my inner Loki playing chess while Audra is playing checkers.

"It's not what you think," I say. "It's not that she hasn't moved on. She just didn't want to upstage your wedding with our news."

"Your what?" Audra's eyes widen.

I squeeze Talia's hand, telling her to play along. "We're engaged."

Audra's jaw drops. "You're *what*?"

Kyle scoffs and turns away, swearing. I only wish I'd thought of this play sooner.

"Yeah, and when we visited my family last month, they wanted Talia to be in our family pictures since she's my fiancée. I think Talia just feels torn because of that."

"I do." Talia nods her agreement. "It wouldn't be right for me to be in the pictures without my fiancé."

"Okay." Audra furrows her brow, considering. "Then I guess—"

"Don't say it, Audra," Kyle barks. "Do not fucking say what I think you're about to say."

She ignores him. "Then I guess Lucien will need to be in the pictures, too."

"Jesus Christ!" Kyle puts his hands on his head, coming unglued. "No fucking way am I letting that happen."

Talia squeezes my hand. We're lucky we get to see such a dramatic performance without even having to pay for tickets. And it's starring the two most deserving people I know.

Audra approaches Kyle, and even though she's trying to talk quietly, we can still hear her. "I'm in charge of the wedding details, remember? You said you'd marry me in Antarctica if I wanted."

Kyle's seething. "I'd rather do that than have Lucien motherfucking Beaumont in our wedding photos."

"Well, you want your kid-diddling stepbrother in our photos, so I get to have my sister and her fiancé."

"Holy shit," Talia whispers.

"Real nice, announcing that about Greg to everyone." Kyle wipes his bleeding cheek with his hand.

Audra holds his gaze, her steeliness reminding me of Talia. "Fuck kid diddlers, Kyle. Everyone should know he's a perv who hid cameras in a dance studio bathroom."

"Jesus," Kayla says. "Is he allowed to be at this wedding? Will there be kids?"

"No kids," Audra seethes. "I had to tell all my friends and family no kids, all because of Kyle's registered sex offender cousin."

Things are spiraling even further out of control than I hoped for.

"Fine," Kyle grinds out. "Talia's boy toy can be in the goddamn pictures."

"Good!" Audra brightens, her smile a little scary. "Then it's settled. And you two are going to be brothers-in-law, so you'd better find a way to get along. Now let's finish this scavenger hunt. The photographer will be waiting for us at the end."

Talia and I linger, letting the others resume the hike. As soon as they're out of earshot, she throws herself at me in a hug, burying her face in my shoulder to muffle her laughter.

"You're an evil genius," she says in my ear. "I

thought this trip would be hell, but instead we're making core memories I'll love for the rest of my life."

"I thought your sister was gonna lose it," I say in her ear.

"She gets stressed out about things being perfect."

I chuckle softly. "Then she's in for a lifetime of disappointment with Macintire."

"You're the best, Lucien." She pulls back and meets my eyes, her gaze warm. "I mean it. You've been the most amazing friend to me on this trip. I'll never forget it."

A friend. After all this, she still thinks of me as just a friend. I don't let my disappointment show.

"We should catch up," I say.

She falls into step beside me and we return to our hike, the view of a black sand beach like nothing I've ever seen before.

I thought we were both feeling something, but now I don't know. Maybe it's just me.

# CHAPTER FIFTEEN

Talia

Something wakes me up from a deep sleep. I shift and sit up, Lucien getting out of bed.

"When is it?" I ask, groggy from sleeping so deeply at last.

He grins at me, his left eye black and swollen. "It's morning. Someone's at the door."

Shit. It's Kyle and Audra's wedding day. I'm not dreading it as much as I was before we got here, but I still want to get it behind me.

Lucien's been sleeping in lightweight blue cotton pants, and I enjoy the last few seconds of his bare chest as he pulls on a white T-shirt.

"Are you answering it?" I panic, pulling the covers up to my neck.

We have a suite, so whoever's at the front door won't be able to see me in bed unless Lucien lets them in.

"It might be important," he says. "Maybe the wedding got called off because Kyle's been cheating."

I choke out a note of laughter and unscrew the cap from the bottle of water on my bedside table. Whoever's at the door, I don't feel like seeing them. Since I can get there without being seen from the doorway to our room, I hurry into the bathroom and turn on the shower.

It's almost seven thirty a.m. That means this will all be over in twelve hours. Lucien and I can make a quick appearance at the reception, get sloppy on top-shelf shit at the open bar Kyle's paying for, and then move on.

As I massage coconut-scented shampoo into my scalp, I think about the closure today should bring. I've been wallowing in self-pity for too long. Their marriage is the last chapter in this saga. It means I need to stop feeling sorry for myself and get a job. Save enough money to move out of my dad's.

It's time for me to make a new life for myself. I don't know where or what that will look like. Since I'm adamant about my job requirements, I may have to move far to find the right fit. I only want to work with disabled people. And it has to include body movement and the ability to build a program I'm passionate about.

I'm not moving back to California. I'll cede the entire state to Kyle and Audra. But I'm open to anywhere else.

When I met Lucien Beaumont that night at Lucky's, I had no idea how important he'd become to me. I'm used to seeing him and his teammates almost every day. I've truly loved helping out with my dad's team. It can't last forever, though.

I finish my shower, brush my teeth and look at myself in the mirror for a few seconds.

I can do this. Lucien will be with me. I'll find a way to get one of those photos of Kyle after he got stung by the jellyfish and he was throwing a tantrum, and I'll have it made into a giant canvas to hang in my next home.

Even though I've moved on, I'm human. My group text with Suki, Mara and Lainey has reminded me that it's okay to call out the shittiness of this situation. Even if I seem petty. Even if I am petty. Having friends who get it and defend me as fiercely as I do has made me stand up a little straighter. No matter where I end up, they'll always be my friends.

I grab my pink terry cloth robe from a hook in

the bathroom and put it on, my mind wandering to what eye makeup I'm going to wear today.

When I step back into the bedroom, I inhale deeply, taking in the scent of coffee. And vinegar. This room may smell like vinegar for a long time after the amount we went through yesterday washing Lucien's stings.

He's lying in bed, looking at his phone.

"Who was it?" I ask.

"Your sister."

"What did she want?"

He sighs softly. "She wanted to drop off a bridesmaid dress in case you changed your mind."

"What the fuck? I'm never changing my mind."

"I know. I argued with her for a solid five minutes."

"I don't see the dress, so you must've won."

He arches his brows. "It's sitting on the floor in the hallway."

"The dress?"

"Yeah. She threw it into the room, so I threw it back."

"Nice."

I reach up to unwrap the towel from my hair, my robe opening a little in front as I do. Lucien's eyes are locked onto me, his expression longing. I've never felt a look like I do this one. I feel it in my pounding heart. In my swirling stomach. Between my thighs.

"What does that look mean?"

I want to hear him say it. He makes me feel more desirable than any man ever has without even saying a word. But when he does use words, it lights me up from the inside out.

"You know what it means." He gestures at his tented erection. "It means I want you."

I laugh lightly. "Well, I'm the only available woman, so ..."

He gets out of bed, pursing his lips and narrowing his eyes. I'm taken aback. Is he...angry?

I can hardly breathe as he paces toward me, commanding every last shred of my focus. When he reaches me, his hands deftly untie the knot in my robe's belt, and then he opens it, a shiver passing through my entire body.

He rakes his gaze down my body and back up to my face, his dark eyes stealing my breath and making me forget all inhibition.

"This is perfection." His voice has an edge of gruffness that turns me on hard. "These"—he cups one of my breasts, his thumb grazing my hardened nipple—"are flawless. You're so sexy, Talia, and you have no idea."

He runs the backs of his fingers down my midriff, making me gasp. When he slides one hand between my thighs and lightly cups me, I make a sound that's part moan, part sigh.

"I told you to make me work for it." His eyes are locked onto mine. "Is that what this is? Are you making me work for it, or do you not want me like I want you? So much it takes every ounce of self-control to keep my hands off you."

He puts his other hand on one side of my neck, his thumb grazing my jawline. It's possessive, and I whimper without even realizing I'm doing it.

"I want you, too," I whisper.

It's not wise. Downright careless. Borderline dangerous. But I need him to keep touching me. Nothing else matters. This is a moment of raw honesty. We're both stripped bare, and I don't feel self-conscious.

This feeling surging through me is power. Soul-deep arousal. I don't care about anything or anyone but him right now. This.

I shrug my shoulders, letting my robe fall to the floor. We lunge for each other at the same time, my mouth crashing against his as he wraps his hands around my waist.

Our kiss is hungry and demanding, his groan making me want to climb him. When he pulls my body tightly against his, his erection presses against my core and I gasp. The feeling of his clothes on my hypersensitive bare skin is bliss.

He steps back suddenly, the air cold where his body was just a second ago. "You want this, right? I need you to tell me you want this."

"Yes, can't you tell?"

The corners of his lips tug up and he gets on his knees. "I want you every goddamn day, Talia. I want you when I wake up." He kisses the skin just above the curls of my bikini line. "I want you when I'm practicing." Another kiss, right next to the first one. "I want you when I'm driving." Another kiss, and I wind my fingers into his hair and tug it. "When I'm with you." His lips move lower and I gasp. "When I'm not." He looks up at me, his eyes swimming with desire. "All the time."

"I want you, too," I confess. "Even when I'm fighting it, I still want you."

He stands, lifting me by the waist. I wrap my legs around him and he carries me to the bed, kissing me all the way.

When he puts a knee on the mattress and gently lowers me to it, I part my legs, my body craving a deeper connection with his. He brushes the hair from my forehead and asks, "Still yes?"

I nod, putting a hand behind his neck and pulling him toward me. "Fuck yes."

He kisses one of my nipples, then sucks it into his mouth. I close my eyes, lost in sensation. It's the first time in my life my mind has been completely shut off. There's no thinking, just feeling.

When he's lined up at my entrance, I push his lower back, urging him on. He sinks into me and my cry mingles with his groan. His eyes seek reassurance from mine that it's not too much, and I say, "Don't stop. Give me more."

And he does. He thrusts all the way in, filling me completely and then some. It doesn't hurt, though. The sheer satisfaction on his face makes me high. I grind against him and we become one, our bodies in sync.

He buries his face in my neck, his scruff brushing my skin as he kisses me. All he's ever done for me is give. He gives and gives and asks nothing in return. I love knowing he's finally taking, even though he's still giving at the same time.

He's Lucien, though, and he won't let himself come until I do. He slows, getting up on his knees so he can rub his thumb over my clit as he fucks me. My ankles are over his shoulders and he kisses my calf. It's a sweet, tender kiss that contrasts with his deep, hard thrusts into me.

"Oh god." My lips part and my eyes find his. "I'm close. Keep doing ... oh, fuck. Yes."

I fist the bedsheet as I unravel, his name a cry that's almost spiritual. His expression is strained as he holds on until I'm coming down, and then he finally lets go. I can't look away from his face as he comes inside me, the high of making him feel this way a drug I could get addicted to fast. He stills and then goes slack, exhaling hard.

"How's that for a good friend?" He smiles and kisses me softly.

"Unreal. And you know there's been an underlying ... something sexual since the night we met."

He moves off me, resting on one hip and running his fingertips over my stomach. "Hell yeah, I do. You were the one denying it."

"I didn't know ..." I'm not sure how to put it into words. "That it could be like this. I've never had something like this."

"Me neither."

I grin, reaching up to finally run my hand over the hair on his muscled chest. "I'm not even freaking out about the wedding anymore. Let's do this. Hopefully everyone will be able to tell how freshly fucked we are."

"Oh, don't worry, I'm gonna tell everyone. I'll see if the pastor will let me have the floor before the ceremony starts."

That makes me laugh. "Please don't. You being in the family wedding photos is more than enough fun for today."

He gives me a wicked grin. "We'll see about that."

# CHAPTER SIXTEEN

Lucien

TALIA'S LIPS quirk into a smile as I use the tip of my index finger to slowly trace out the letters of a message on her leg, just above her knee. I started doing it to distract her from the wedding ceremony, but now it's turned into something fun.

I've spelled out each letter of I-W-A-N-T-T-O-L-I-C-K-Y-O-U-R-P-U, when she bites her lips and covers my hand with hers, stopping me. Her lips are pulling into a smile.

Coach Turner is sitting on her other side, his arms crossed and his expression stoic. He's at the end of our pew, right next to the aisle he walked Audra down. He did his duty as her father, but when Kyle reached out to shake his hand, Coach glared at him and walked away. It was savage as fuck. He refused to sit up front with the other family members, walking almost all the way back down the aisle to sit near the back of the church with me and Talia.

Audra was so adamant about no one taking photos with their phones that an usher confiscated them before we were allowed to come in. But I would have loved a picture of Macintire standing there with his hand out, his lower lip swollen and cut and his right eye black and blue.

"Kyle, from the moment we met, I knew you were the one," Audra says, getting choked up on the first sentence of her vows.

Coach shifts in his seat and exhales through his nose, and Talia hums a note of amusement, likely because he was with Talia when Audra met him.

Everything about this ceremony has been awkward. People have been looking at Talia and whispering, and even though she's been ignoring it, I know she has to be aware of it.

She looks sexy as hell in her off-white strapless dress, the sides of her hair styled up in a big, loose bun while the rest is loose around her shoulders. When we walked into the church, she was a picture of grace and confidence, but I could feel her shaking when I put my arm around her.

The hard part is almost over, though. I never would have thought the day I went to Kyle Douchebag Macintire's wedding would be the best day of my life, but it is.

I didn't want to leave our room this morning. Not just because the sex was incredible—and it was—but because of the intimacy of lying beside Talia in bed afterward. Both of us were naked, our legs tangled together as we whispered to each other, confessing all the times we wanted each other. Her laugh is my favorite sound in the world. It's rich and unreserved, and bringing it out of her is second only to bringing her to an orgasm that makes her cry out my name.

I'll be doing that again later. I've only gotten the tiniest taste of her, and I'm starving for more.

"Audra Turner, you complete me." Kyle's start to his vows makes the maid of honor roll her eyes.

What a cheese fest. Audra had an entire app designed for this three-day shitshow. It includes the schedule for every day, stupid stories about Audra and Kyle falling in love, and fake-ass photos of them gazing into each other's eyes. I don't have the app on my phone, but Talia does, so she can access the schedule. And it's borderline aggressive about telling people to use the official hashtag of #MacintirelyIn-Love in every social media post.

Talia was so amused the first time she saw it that she snort-laughed.

I glance at her, and I can tell she's mentally elsewhere. Hopefully thinking about the sex we had earlier, because I sure as hell have been. I kiss her bare shoulder softly, and she smiles at me.

Finally, the pastor declares them Mr. and Mrs. Shitface, at least in my head. They're dismissing everyone aisle by aisle, but we file out before they get to us.

As soon as we step outside into the warm, breezy air, Coach Turner gives me a relieved look, then turns his attention to Talia.

"Still up for the reception?" he asks her. "We can skip it if you want."

"Nah. Kyle's paying for an open bar. Let's go drink the best alcohol money can buy."

"Attagirl," he says.

We fly out late tomorrow morning, and something tells me we're all going to wish we were staying an extra day to recover from today.

---

"ALL I WANT for my birthday and Christmas and"— Talia furrows her brow, concentrating—"my birthday forever is a thumb drive with those photos on it."

She's had more than a few drinks, and so has Coach Turner. The reception venue has a bar, and we've taken over three stools at one end. Turner's had several shots, and he's actually smiling and laughing as we talk about the wedding photos.

Audra wanted photos of just her, Kyle and their parents, and then photos of just them and their siblings and their partners. Of course, as Talia's supposed fiancé, I was in that one. I was also in the one with every family member from both families, grinning like the happiest motherfucker on the planet.

Kyle sulked the entire time. Audra's still behaving like a coked-out bridezilla, micromanaging every last detail she can. Talia, Coach and I are on a down-hill slide, though—enjoying the last of our time here, but glad we're leaving tomorrow.

"I'll see what I can do," Coach tells Talia in response to her request for the photos with me in them.

Fortunately, Talia had prepared him for hearing that we're engaged. He wasn't thrilled, even knowing it's not real, but he tolerated it. Now he's tipping back his glass tumbler, getting the last few drops of whiskey from it.

"That's it for me," he says. "I said I'd stay through the toasts and they're about to start."

Talia bursts out laughing from just the sight of

Kayla taking the microphone from the DJ to do her maid of honor toast. She's been outdrinking both me and Coach, and I'm kind of worried about her since I've never known her to drink much.

"Hey everyone, thanks for your attention," Kayla says. "Audra and I were college roommates and I just want to offer up my warmest wishes for this happy couple. Cheers."

It's the most underwhelming toast ever. Talia downs a shot of tequila instead of drinking from the flutes of champagne that were passed out, and when she slams the shot glass on the bar, she lets out a little burp and laughs.

I shake my head, knowing there won't be any more sex for us today. I'll be surprised if she makes it back to our room before she passes out. It's more likely I'll be carrying her there.

Kyle's best man is one of his high school hockey teammates, and he spends more time talking about how cool it is that Kyle's a pro hockey player than he does about him and Audra.

I turn to make sure Talia is still upright on her barstool, and she's gone. I lock eyes with Coach, both of us finding her at the same time.

"If I could have your attention for one more toast!" Talia has one hand wrapped around an invisible microphone and the other one in the air, her index finger raised. "Just one!"

Oh shit. She's not yelling, but she's not *not* yelling, either. She's standing between two tables full of reception guests, too far away for me to intervene without everyone seeing.

"Hey, hi! I'm Talia Turner, Audra's sister. Well, I'm also Kyle's ex, but everyone knows that. Everyone! It's why you've all been looking at me all day, right? Right?"

Coach Turner cringes, walking over to her.

"I'm doing a toast, Dad!" She walks away from him, moving closer to the dance floor set up in the middle of the room. "So where was I?" She taps the invisible microphone. "Is this thing on? Anyway! Like I was saying, it's so funny that my sister knew Kyle was THE ONE"—she makes air quotes with the hand she's not using for the invisible microphone—"because I was already dating him then!" She looks at her sister and Kyle, who are sitting at the head table with the same horrified expression. "Auds, you should have mentioned that you planned to fuck him behind my back. And also! He used that 'you complete me' bullshit he STOLE from a movie on me too."

She stumbles slightly and I'm torn about whether I should let her keep going or go end this.

"But don't feel bad for me!" she yells. "Seriously, do not. I'm so good. I'm with a man now. A real man!

One who doesn't need me to spank him so he can come when he's drunk."

There's a ripple of soft, stunned laughter.

The best man approaches her, putting his hands on her shoulders. Coach Turner and I both go toward them at the same time.

"Don't touch me!" She shakes him off. "I wasn't ready. To be done, I mean. It's Kyle, you guys! Kyle wanted me to spank him so he could come when he was drunk. But Lucien—he's nothing like Kyle. He gives and gives. I mean, I fucking *love him*. It's like ... no one's ever actually *had* me. Not the way he does."

I stop at the edge of the dance floor. Coach is there, too. Audra is crying into her hands at the head table.

"Anyway, here's to a lifetime of spanking him, Audra!" Talia raises an invisible glass in the air. "Unless he cheats on you, too. Or maybe you'll cheat on him? I don't know. Either way, you deserve each other!"

Coach puts an arm around her shoulders, easing her away from the dance floor.

"What? You didn't like my toast?" she says.

The room is completely silent, other than the sound of Audra's wailing, everyone looking at Talia. The expressions of pity and disbelief make me fucking furious.

"She's drunk," a woman at the table next to me says, sneering.

"You would be too, if you were her," I snap.

"Oh god," Talia's saying as Coach leads her off the dance floor. "I really just did that?"

I go to her and put my arm around her shoulders. She buries her face in my chest, shielding her face. I lead her away from the tables and out of the room as quickly as I can.

"I'm going to be sick," she says weakly.

"Let's get her into a cold shower," Coach says, taking off his suit jacket as he follows me.

"I'll do it."

He lowers his brows. "I shouldn't have let her drink so much. She never drinks like that."

"I should've stopped her, too."

Talia stands up straight and looks between the two of us. She shakes her head and groans.

"Don't worry about it," I tell her. "We're going back to our room."

"I want to make sure you get her there okay," Coach says.

"I've got her." I meet his eyes. "I promise I've got her."

He nods. "Okay. Text me later and let me know how she's doing, okay?"

"I will."

The reception venue is also our hotel, so I hustle

Talia onto an elevator. I don't want anyone coming out of that reception to confront her.

She puts a hand on the elevator wall when it starts moving, looking confused.

"It's an elevator, babe," I say. "You're fine."

"We had sex."

I grin at the way she's acting like she just realized it for the first time. "Yeah, we did."

"Lucien. What did I say back there?"

I shrug. "Not much. Just like 'congratulations' and stuff like that."

She cringes and takes a deep breath in and out. "I'm going to be sick."

"Hold it in for two minutes if you can."

The elevator doors slide open on our floor, and I lead the way to our room. I manage to get her into the room, but before I can get her dress unzipped, she bolts for the bathroom to barf into the toilet.

I wet a washcloth and pass it to her when she's done.

"Just leave me here to die," she says mournfully.

"You're not gonna die," I assure her. "You'll just feel like you're going to for the next day or so."

She curls up on the tile floor of the bathroom, her only answer a weak groan.

# CHAPTER SEVENTEEN

Talia

It would be bad enough if I had only humiliated myself by yelling a drunken toast into an invisible microphone last night. If my attempt at taking the high road had crashed and burned spectacularly in front of three hundred twenty-five guests at my sister and Kyle's wedding.

Today, though, it's worse. Someone took a video of it and posted it on social media, and now hundreds of thousands of people have witnessed me belting out things I never, ever would have said without doing all those shots.

Lucien is beside me in the backseat of the SUV

taking us to the airport. The itinerary in the app listed a brunch this morning at ten a.m. for close friends and family, but I wouldn't have shown up there for anything.

Dad's flight left around that time, and we were supposed to be on the same flight. Lucien booked us an extra day at the resort and moved our flight to evening instead of morning so I could sleep. And so we could sneak out of the resort while Audra, Kyle, their wedding party and families were at the farewell luau several miles away.

I still feel like I've been run over by a fleet of trucks. I can't get rid of my crushing headache, and I haven't been able to eat. I'm not complaining, though, because I was so stupid for drinking so much. I deserve to have the mother of all hangovers.

I'm horrified as I watch myself walk toward the dance floor on my phone for at least the tenth time in the past hour, AirPods tucked into my ears.

This time, I scroll the comments.

*ABSOLUTE FUCKING LEGEND!*

*Will someone come help get my jaw off the floor???*

*This is just mean. Her sister shouldn't have stolen her man, I'm not saying that's right. But this isn't right, either.*

*That mf groom just pissed his pants fr...*

*OOF. They done FAFO!*

*Get to work, Internet. Who is this? And more importantly, who's Lucien???*

I TURN my phone over in my lap, unable to even look at Lucien. After everything he's done for me, now he's going to get dragged into this sideshow. We should have been having more incredible sex last night, but instead, he had to talk me into sitting in the bathtub for a cold shower while I was crying hysterically about my family never speaking to me again.

It was a hellish night. He was worried at one point that I might have alcohol poisoning, but I was sobered up enough by then to assure him I didn't have any of the symptoms.

I've never puked so much or felt so miserable. Leaving the resort felt like a walk of shame.

"What row are we in for the flight home?" I ask him.

I'm wondering if we were able to keep our first-class seats with the flight change, but I feel like an asshole asking.

"I don't remember." He takes my hand, kissing the back of it. "You hanging in there?"

I nod and smile weakly.

I said I love him. All the truths I'm afraid to say out loud came gushing out of me last night, like a fire hose with no one holding on to it.

Even though I've moved on, I do resent my sister saying she knew Kyle was the one as soon as she saw him. And him? He's not even sorry. Audra has told me many times that she's sorry for what she did. Kyle has never once said anything indicating he thinks I deserved better.

Lucien shows up for me. I didn't realize what that was like until I experienced it. He cares if I'm comfortable and happy. He cares if people treat me badly, and he calls them out on it. Kyle's swollen lip and black eye are proof of that.

"How are you feeling?" I ask him.

"Not as bad as this morning. I'm not used to doing that many shots anymore."

The skin around his eye is a darker shade of purple today. He's wearing a Crush baseball hat, a plain gray T-shirt and black sweats, and he looks good.

"My IG inbox is getting flooded," he says.

I cover my eyes with my hand. "I'm sorry. That's my fault."

"Nah. I'll warn you, though, the guys are going crazy over your speech. They're pretty stoked."

I scoff and smile. "Suki and Mara are all over me

to talk about it. I told them I'm not there yet. Maybe when my head doesn't feel like a grenade just exploded inside of it."

"Isaac's picking us up in Cleveland."

"My dad can pick us up."

He shakes his head slightly. "Isaac's doing it."

I furrow my brow. "What aren't you telling me?"

"It's nothing major."

"Lucien. What is it?"

"There are photographers at your dad's place, and at mine. Isaac's borrowing a van with tinted windows to get us to his house."

I bury my face in my hands. "This just goes from bad to worse to so much fucking worse."

He pats my knee. "It won't last, Tal. When they don't get what they want, they'll move on."

"Does Isaac live at a fraternity house?"

He grins. "It has a frat house vibe for sure. There's never TP in the bathroom and his living room has a bunch of pinball machines in it."

"Awesome."

"It'll all die down soon."

"I'm sorry about all this."

His expression turns serious. "Stop saying that. This will blow over."

"I ruined their reception. Even after everything they've done, I didn't want to ruin anything."

"You didn't ruin it. I'm sure it kept rolling after we left."

A sick sensation rolls through my stomach. "And now I've screwed myself. I'm internet famous for getting drunk and ranting about spanking my ex. Right when I need to start applying for jobs. People will see me and be like, *Oh, it's that crazy woman from the wedding.*"

The SUV stops at the airport entrance, and the driver comes around to open my door. Lucien passes him a tip and gets our bags.

"Our airline is this way," I say, pointing. "Or did we have to switch airlines?"

"Yeah, we switched airlines. Just follow me."

———

"Are you serious?"

Thirty minutes later, I gape at Lucien as he leads me toward a small, private luxury airplane.

"It was just the right timing. You know Hunter Beck?"

"I know of him, but I've never met him. He's the billionaire who plays for Pittsburgh, right?"

"Yep. He's a friend, and he's spending the break at his place in Kauai. His plane can get us home and get back here in time for his flight back."

My shoulders sink with relief. "That's really nice

of him. I was thinking we might be in coach and not even sitting next to each other, with the last-minute flight change."

He grins. "Hunter's your friend now, too. He also hates Macintire, and he said to tell you, 'great fucking speech.'"

I smile weakly. "I'm probably uninvited from every family function for the rest of my life, so I'm not looking for compliments on it."

"Your dad's got your back, and he's your family. And I'm not trying to be mean, but I don't think you're missing much with your mom and sister."

I sigh heavily. "Yeah. I kind of want to start my job search in other countries, so I can get a fresh start somewhere new."

He pinches his brows together, concerned. "Other countries?"

I cringe, realizing my mistake. "I didn't mean ... we need to talk about it. I don't know that there will be a job opening for me in the Cleveland area."

"That doesn't mean you need to move to another fucking country."

We're waiting on the tarmac, and a woman walks down the plane's stairs. Lucien walks toward her and I follow, regretting the way I told him I might need to move away.

"Mr. Beaumont?"

The flight attendant looks like a model, her body tight and toned and her smile flawless.

"Lucien." He shakes her hand.

"And you must be Miss Turner." She extends her hand to me and I shake it.

"Talia," I say.

"I'm Kate, and I'll be taking care of you on today's flight. Are you ready to board?"

"Yeah, we're all set," Lucien says.

We follow her up the plane's stairs, and then we set foot into a more luxurious plane interior than I've ever imagined. There are big leather seats, a few with views of TV screens, and a separate bedroom with a queen-size bed layered with a crisp white comforter, soft blankets and velvet pillows in a deep navy blue.

Our conversation is forgotten as we settle in, Kate bringing us water and snacks. I turn the power off on my phone and tuck it into my bag, promising I'll spend less time on it for the next few weeks.

I'm embarrassed by my behavior yesterday, but I'm not going to keep watching the video and reading the comments. I need to move on. Put it behind me. Focus on the rest of my life.

Which I hope includes Lucien. I have to find a job, and I don't know how I can work in my field and also see him regularly, considering his travel schedule.

There are so many unanswered questions. It's overwhelming to think about them while my head is throbbing and I feel like walking death.

For now, I just want to get back to Cleveland. Our trip here was a lot more eventful than I expected.

# CHAPTER EIGHTEEN

Lucien

TALIA GRAZES her fingertips up and down my chest, going a little bit lower each time. It feels so amazing that I pretend I'm still asleep, waiting for her to reach my cock.

Her breath is warm on the shell of my ear. When she finally gets her hand where I want it, I can't help groaning.

We've been lying low at Isaac's for the past couple of days, and this afternoon, we have to return to reality.

Coach gave us the morning off, but we're practicing this afternoon and we have a home game tomorrow. I only have a few more hours of being mostly alone with Talia all day, every day.

Isaac's been here, of course, since it's his house. But we have a bedroom to ourselves, even if it's nothing more than a queen-size bed. That's all we really need, anyway. Our stuff is piled up on the floor.

"I want you," Talia whispers in my ear.

My lips quirk with a smile. "I couldn't tell."

She nips at my earlobe. "I'll take care of myself if I need to."

I turn to face her. "The fuck you will."

She smiles, her hair messy and her skin natural, without a bit of makeup. This is how I like her best. Only I get to see her this way, and I plan to keep it that way.

I slide my hand beneath the T-shirt she sleeps in, which is one of mine that I packed for our trip. Isaac offered to loan her some of his clothes, and I just laughed. Over my dead body will she wear another man's clothes. I'll go naked so she can wear mine if I have to.

Suki dropped off some clothes for both of us, but Talia slipped into my shirt before bed our first night here, and I don't want her to sleep in anything else now.

When I cup one of her breasts and tease her nipple, she moans softly.

She must finally be feeling better. That hangover really took her down. Yesterday, she spent a lot of time curled up on Isaac's couch, reading a book on her phone. She ate a can of chicken noodle soup, but that was it.

I texted Isaac on our flight home and told him no talking about the toast, the video, or anything else about the wedding or our trip. He's been good about it.

Within two minutes of putting my hands under her shirt, Talia is squeezing my ass, urging me to get on top of her. When she wants sex, she doesn't like waiting, and I like that about her.

I kiss her neck, her moans becoming more insistent. When I kiss her cheek, her nose, and her forehead, she squeezes my ass so hard her nails dig in, and I arch my brows.

"You want me bad, huh?"

She smiles. "My headache is finally gone. You've got fifteen seconds to get your cock inside me, or I'm getting on top of you."

I kiss her lips lightly, humming with amusement. "You can try."

"If you don't want to fuck me, I can always go see if Isaac will," she says playfully.

I scoff. "Don't make me beat the shit out of my own goalie. Your dad wouldn't like that."

She wrinkles her nose. "Not a good time to mention him."

"Sorry about that." I move on top of her, lacing my hands through her fingers on both hands and pinning them to her pillow. "I'll make it up to you."

"I look forward to it."

Her eyes are like an abstract painting. They're a swirl of amber, warm browns and earthy greens. I want to wake up to this view of her every day.

"I love you, Talia. I don't know if you're ready to say it when you're sober, but it doesn't matter. When you're looking for a job and deciding where to move, I want you to know I'm in love with you. I don't want anyone else."

She gently squeezes my hands. "I love you, too. I didn't even realize it was happening, but you've become my closest friend, and you also happen to be incredible in bed. It's a killer combo."

I get to my knees and fist my cock, sliding the crotch of her panties aside. Then I line the tip of my cock up and bury myself all the way inside her with one hard thrust.

"Oh, fuck," she cries, gasping. "That feels good."

"You're going to have some wet panties after this, love. Not just from your hot pussy, but from my cum."

Her eyes brighten with desire and she pants, "Yes."

I put my hands on the backs of her thighs and push them forward, driving into her again.

"Fuck me hard," she whispers. "Make me come, baby."

Her words are like a drug, my body responding to her without thought. I'm fucking feral for the way she looks and sounds, spread open to me, her cheeks rosy and her round tits bouncing hard as I plow into her over and over. I want her to call me *baby* every day. On the phone. Over breakfast, when I bring her a fresh cup of coffee. But especially when I'm fucking her like this.

She arches her back and her lips round into a silent O of pleasure. She's got a thing about Isaac not hearing her orgasm.

Not me. I want him to tell every member of my team—or better, every man on the planet—that she's mine now. I groan hard as I pump my hips into her one last time, filling her pussy.

"God, you're amazing," she says when I pull out of her a few seconds later.

"You bring it out of me." I move onto my back and she curls against my side, her fingertip back on my chest, making a slow circle.

"I don't want to get out of this bed," she says softly.

"We don't have to." I brush the hair away from her eyes with my fingers. "At least not yet."

"I like this world. Just us. Let's live here for a little bit longer."

I pull the covers over us and try not to think about her applying for jobs in other states.

---

"THANKS FOR BREAKING your dick off in my ass, cocksucker!" Isaac yells at the TV.

It's an hour later, and the smell of brewing coffee got me and Talia out of bed. We came down to find Isaac had been up all night playing *Call of Duty* with his online gaming friends.

He has dark circles beneath his eyes and his coffee table is crowded with empty energy drink cans, dirty dishes and open chip bags. Some of the stuff has been on the coffee table since we got here a couple days ago. Isaac is not a good housekeeper, and that's putting it mildly.

Talia is currently loading dishes from yesterday into the dishwasher.

"Hey. You don't need to clean his house, babe," I say.

"I can't look at these any longer," she gripes. "They're about to grow legs and walk away."

"What the fuck, man?" Isaac yells. "Are you new here?"

Talia shakes her head. "He's a fourteen-year-old

trapped in a twenty-six-year-old's body. Does he bring women here?"

"I have no idea."

"He's the kind of guy who offers to cook you dinner and then microwaves a couple of Hot Pockets."

"Hot Pockets are delicious!" Isaac yells from the other room. "Don't walk in here for the next minute, I'm pissing in a Gatorade bottle."

Talia makes a face. Isaac refuses to leave his matches to use the bathroom, so he pisses in empty bottles while he's playing. It's disgusting.

"I don't care if there are photographers outside your place, we're staying there tonight," Talia says.

"Yep." I glance at my watch. "Isaac, we have to leave for practice in five minutes."

"Yeah, I'm ready."

Talia looks at me over her shoulder. "I'm staying here to clean this place."

"Don't. It'll be a mess again in a few days."

She shrugs a shoulder. "Probably. But I've got nervous energy, and I feel like cleaning."

Yesterday, she called her dad and told him she won't be coming to help out with the team anymore. She doesn't want to bring any negative attention on us from the viral video. He said he understands, and that even though she's welcome to stay with him as long as she wants, he's glad she's ready to move forward and look for a job.

I'm not. I'd prefer she move in with me, but I know she wouldn't be happy just being my live-in girlfriend.

It sounds perfect to me, having her waiting in my bed when I get home late from road trips, and looking for her in the stands or the boxes at home games, wearing my jersey.

I don't want to come on too strong, though. My mom wrote me a letter when she knew she was going to die, and I've read it dozens of times. She told me the right woman won't cling to me and expect us to do everything together. She'll have her own friends and interests. Her own career and hobbies. That's the key to a lasting relationship, she said. Both of you leaving the bubble of your relationship. Trusting the other person is doing what they want and need to be happy and healthy. And then coming back together to hear about the other person's life outside the relationship, and spending time together.

My mom was wise. I miss her every day, but her letter helps me feel like she's still with me. She knew what challenges and choices life would throw at me.

She'd love Talia. Mom volunteered with Special Olympics because one of her close friends had a son who was part of it, and she loved it so much that she kept volunteering. She'd light up if she could talk to Talia about her work, and she'd approve of the way Talia shut my shit down the night we met.

"Feel like going out for dinner tonight?" I ask Talia.

"Yes, I'm over being cooped up and eating delivery food."

I stand behind her, wrapping my arms around her waist. "Are you sure you don't want to come on one last road trip?"

She relaxes back against my chest, sighing. "I want to, but with the video, I don't think I should."

"People are overwhelmingly in support of you. You'll get more requests for autographs than anyone on the team."

She groans. "A drunken tirade isn't something to sign autographs for. I'm planning to hang out with Suki tomorrow. Charlotte is in a school play in the evening, and we're going to it."

"Good. I'm sure Carter hates that he can't be there."

Talia fits in so well with my Crush family. I always envied what Carter and Suki have, and if Talia stays close by, I think we could end up with a life like theirs. Kids, a home, maybe even a giant pet pig who destroys the floors and hogs the couch.

"Don't wear yourself out cleaning up after Isaac."

"I won't. Seriously, I don't mind. I'm doing our laundry, too."

I reluctantly step away from her. "Then I guess this is where we stop being together twenty-four seven."

She smiles at me over her shoulder. "Absence makes the heart grow fonder."

"It also makes the dick grow harder."

"I'll never complain about that." She turns and leans up to kiss me. "Have a good practice."

"I'll see you back at my place, babe."

I walk into the living room, where Isaac is still immersed in his game.

"I'm not gonna be late for practice, and I don't have my car here, so get off your lazy ass and let's go."

He flicks a glare at me. "Fine." A couple seconds pass. "I have to go, guys. My asshole friend is making me go to work."

"You got a whole week off from your head injury. You should've been rehabbing over the break."

He takes off his headset and sets it next to him on the couch. "I did. It's just not the only thing I did."

I gesture at the coffee table. "Clearly."

"You're busting my balls a lot for someone who left cum stains all over my guest room."

I shake my head. "Yeah, I shot it all over the walls, dumbass. Let's go."

# CHAPTER NINETEEN

Talia

"I MISS LEO." Mara nibbles the ridged edge of a Reese's peanut butter cup, carefully eating it off first. "He hasn't even been gone for twenty-four hours and I miss him."

"That's sweet," Lainey says.

"A girl gets used to being fucked well before work every morning after a full week of it."

Suki clears her throat. "Children in close proximity."

Mara sighs, using her teeth to scrape the chocolate top off her peanut butter cup. "I'll just fill the void with wine and chocolate, I guess."

"I hope you're using the word void figuratively

and not literally," Suki quips. "Because some voids shouldn't be filled with wine and chocolate. That'll throw your pH right off. Give you a nasty yeast infection."

We're just killing time, sitting in the living room. Waiting for their other friends, Harry and Dex, to get here so we can all leave for Charlotte's school play. She's playing Pepper in *Annie*.

I've met Harry, but I haven't met Dex yet. He's an attorney, like Mara.

"Talia, have you found any jobs you want to apply for?" Lainey asks.

Our group text is very active, and they all know I was planning to look for job openings this morning after Lucien left for the road trip.

"I found two that sound promising. One in Indianapolis and one in Salt Lake City."

"Those are both far away." Suki frowns. "But I get it. You work in a field with limited openings."

"Yeah. I love it here, but there's not a single job opening in my field. There's an athletic trainer job at a community college that I'm qualified for, but it's not what I want."

Darling comes racing into the room. Well, racing for him. It's pretty much just a steady trot. He has a little tiara on his head and what looks like red lipstick on his snout.

"I wasn't done yet!" Hallie, the youngest of the

three girls, comes into the room on his heels, a tube of Chanel lipstick in hand. "Darling Maxwell, get back here."

Darling sits down next to Suki and looks up at her.

"Is that my lipstick?" Suki asks Hallie.

Hallie looks from the lipstick to Suki, and then back at the lipstick again. "I don't know."

Suki arches her brows. "You don't know? Where did you get it?"

"Um ... I think it was in your bathroom."

"It was definitely in my bathroom, because it's mine. That's expensive lipstick, Hals, and it's not meant for Darling."

"Sorry." Hallie turns the tube, lowering the lipstick back into the container.

"Check it for hairs," Suki says. "I don't enjoy picking wiry pig hairs out of my lipstick."

Mara snort-laughs, then covers her mouth.

"We have to go!" Charlotte comes into the room, looking panicked. "I have to be there by six fifteen."

"You will be," Suki promises. "Harry and Dex are less than five minutes away."

It's less than a minute later when the door from the garage into the kitchen opens and Harry walks in, a handsome dark-haired man with him.

"Where's my actress niece?" the man I assume is Dex asks. "I need to get pictures so I can say I saw her first performance when I'm watching her give her Oscars acceptance speech!"

Charlotte smiles. "I'm right here, but take a quick picture because we have to go."

Harry, who is taller than Dex and has lighter hair, is carrying a small box with gold wrapping paper on it. As soon as Dex is finished taking a picture of Charlotte, Harry hands her the box.

"This is from your favorite uncles. We're so proud of you."

Suki gives her two friends a warm look. Carter can't be here tonight, but Suki's friends are making sure Charlotte feels special and loved. I don't know Harry and Dex, but I know I like them.

"Oh!" Charlotte pulls a gold necklace from the box she unwrapped. "It has a theater mask on it. I love it. Thank you."

She hugs them both and Suki gets a picture of them with her between them. Charlotte wants to wear the necklace, so Mara fastens it behind her neck while Suki yells upstairs for the oldest of the girls, Olivia, to come down.

"How long is this going to take?" Olivia asks when she gets downstairs.

Suki gives her a sharp glare and says, "I'm going to pretend you didn't ask that. Get your coats on, girls. It's cold outside."

We all pile into Suki's large SUV, Mara riding

with Harry and Dex. I'm in the back with Charlotte, who asks if she can practice her lines with me.

I say yes, of course. I've never been around a big, happy family like theirs. My mom is nothing like Suki. She was critical of everything. I always looked forward to summers with my dad and Angie, because Angie was nicer than my mom.

"I heard Lucien got stung by jellyfish in Hawaii," Lainey says from the seat in front of mine, turning to face me when Charlotte is finished with her lines. "What was that like?"

"Pretty awful. I had to rinse the stings with vinegar and they hurt for several hours."

"Lucien got stung by jellyfish?" Charlotte gapes at me. "What was he doing?"

"Well, he was swimming in an area with a sign that said not to swim there because of jellyfish."

"Is he dumb?" Hallie asks.

"Hallie!" Suki gives her a shocked look in the rearview mirror.

"It definitely wasn't a smart move," I say, amused. "He knew the risks."

"F-A-F-O," Charlotte says.

"Oh my god." Suki sighs heavily from the driver's seat. "I swear we're good parents, you guys."

She's visibly pregnant. And I'm sure she falls into bed every night after keeping up with three active girls, a huge house, and a pig the size of a small horse. Add a baby to the mix, and she's going to need help sometimes.

Charlotte's school is a sprawling modern brick building. Suki parks and we all go inside, saying goodbye to Charlotte and heading to the school's theater. Since Suki already has tickets, we breeze through the line and find seats near the front.

"I'm so happy for you and Lucien," Lainey says from her seat beside mine. "Bash says he's never seen Lucien so happy. He looks at pictures of you on his phone all the time."

Well, that feels amazing. And it's also a reminder that I should never send him any naughty pics his teammates might see.

"He's really great," I say. "It's weird not being with him all the time anymore."

"What you said about him, you know ... in the video? I teared up when I saw it. Lucien is a good guy, and he deserves someone who gets that and appreciates it."

I hum a note of laughter. "He still wants me after that video was posted, and that says a lot. I really embarrassed myself."

She shrugs. "I don't know. Your sister saying she knew he was the one the first time she saw him? That's an asshole thing to say. You called it out."

"I know, but ... it was unclassy."

"I embarrassed myself once with Bash. I was in high school and he was twenty-one at the time, playing pro hockey. I drove to his house and confessed my longtime love for him. I asked him to my prom."

I cringe. "Oh no."

"I wanted to die, girl. For real. And then my car wouldn't start, so he had to drive me back to Columbus and he told me I was a great girl who would find someone my own age."

"And then later things changed? Obviously."

She nods, grinning. "Yeah. And teenage Lainey was mortified, but now I'm glad I did it. I went big, you know? Not everyone has the courage for that. And then, a few years later, things were different between us."

"I love that. Thank you for sharing it with me."

She covers my hand with hers and squeezes it. "Don't wilt, Talia. I like you just the way you are."

Her words are like a warm blanket being wrapped around me. I hadn't considered that perspective before. My drunken toast was messy and unplanned, but it was authentic. Alcohol gave me the courage to say things I never would have said otherwise.

The lights go down and the play starts. The students' hard work shows, and I'm impressed by every aspect of their performance. Charlotte shines in her role, and her cheering section is the first to its feet for a standing ovation at the end.

Dex gives her a bunch of long-stemmed roses when she finds us at the end of the play. Her sisters tell her how great she was, and her expression reminds me of how my students used to look when I'd tell them how well they did something. It's like water and sun on a dried-out plant.

Harry is hosting a party for the play's entire cast in a private room at his restaurant, and we all get to go, too. His restaurant is spectacular, and Charlotte beams like the star of the show through the entire party. There are even sparkling nonalcoholic drinks in champagne flutes.

I'm checking the score of the game when I can, and I do a little dance when I see that Lucien scored a goal on a power play. As a defenseman, being able to score makes him extra valuable to his team. I feel a pang of wishing I'd been there to see it.

It's still a great night, though. I thought I'd have to force myself to rejoin the world again, but Lucien's team friends are fun to be around, and now they're my friends, too.

I want to keep this. It's so hard to start over in a new place, and I hate the thought of not seeing Lucien and my new friends as much as I do now.

I'm torn between the job I love and the man I've fallen hard for. It's an awful feeling.

"You okay?" Suki asks me, handing me a plate with a piece of chocolate cheesecake garnished with a strawberry slice.

I shake off my worries and smile at her. "I'm good. I'm having a great time."

"I'm so glad you came tonight."

In a perfect world, I could have it all—the job that fulfills me, right here in the place that feels like home now. But that feels impossible.

# CHAPTER TWENTY

Lucien

I TAKE a picture of my plate and send it to Talia with a text.

*Missing you. This is the hotel restaurant's idea of over medium eggs. They're still clucking.*

It's early, so I doubt she's up yet. We landed in Tampa around five hours ago, got a little sleep, and now we're having breakfast before we go to the Tampa arena to prepare for a game tonight.

I'm tired. I haven't been sleeping well on this trip because I miss Talia, and I'm wondering what's going to happen with us.

I got a taste of having her around all the time when she was working with the team. Working for free isn't really working, I guess, and I can't expect her to volunteer forever. Not even if the fringe benefits are worth it.

Deception isn't part of good relationships, but if I didn't care about that, I'd anonymously fund a position for her at a school in Cleveland with the stipulation that they have to hire her.

It's a perfect solution, and probably even tax-deductible, which my accountant would love. But Talia would never trust me again if she found out. I can't risk that.

Bash looks at my plate from the other side of the table and says, "You gonna eat that bacon?"

"Yep."

"What about the eggs?" Isaac says from next to me.

"Help yourself."

He reaches over to my plate and cuts a bite from the eggs. I glare at him.

"Move the fucking eggs to your plate, dipshit. We're not sharing mine."

"Is it that time of the month, you cranky bitch?"

Bash huffs a laugh. "Reasons why Isaac doesn't have a girlfriend, exhibit eighty-seven."

Isaac arches his brows. "Shit, man. I'd never say that to a woman."

"You wouldn't have to say a word to make a woman bolt," I say. "Just take her to your shithole house. There's piss on your bathroom floor and dirty socks everywhere. It smells like a high school boys' locker room."

"That's a weird way to say thanks for letting me crash at your house for a few days, Isaac."

I glare at him. "You know I appreciate it, but hire someone to clean for you. It's not that hard."

He shrugs. "I don't care if my house is spotless."

"Do you care if it gets taken over by rats? That's what happens when you leave food out to rot."

Bash interjects. "Random science fact brought to you by my wife—did you know a group of rats is called a mischief?"

"A better question is, Do I care?"

"Isaac's right, you are a cranky bitch."

Silas laughs from his spot next to Bash. "He's missing his personal assistant."

"Talia's not my personal assistant, she's my girlfriend."

"I know what he's missing, because I had to listen to them going at it for two days straight."

"Seriously?" Preston asks, leaning forward from a few seats over so he can see me. "You and Talia?"

"Me and Talia."

He grins. "Good for you. Don't fuck it up."

When we finish breakfast, we all load onto a bus to go to the arena. This is the grind of pro hockey. There are eighty-two regular-season games every season. This is a quick road trip, and then we'll be home for eight days of home games and practices.

It's sunny and around seventy degrees in Tampa today, but we only get to enjoy it for the walk from the bus into the arena. We start out with our morning skate, and then we have a light practice to run through a few things.

Coach Turner is taking the social media storm over his daughters in stride. He told all of us not to watch any videos about it unless we're on our own time, not to comment about any of it and not to ask him about it.

He doesn't like drama. From what teammates have told me, not only has the attention on Talia over the video not died down, but it's gotten more intense. Now I'm in the mix. With online content creators explaining that Talia was with Kyle until he dumped her for her sister and then she got another hockey player. Like we're all on some soap opera.

When we get back to the visiting team locker room, I check my phone and see that Talia texted me back.

*Those eggs are so runny they could win a marathon. Also, I applied for a job and they called me two hours later asking me to interview. Progress!*

I frown at my screen as I type out a response.

*Great news babe! Where is it?*

*That part's not so great. It's in Salt Lake City.*

"What the fuck?" I set my phone on the bench next to me, frustrated.

"Did the insurance deny your penis enlargement?" Isaac asks with a grin.

I just glare at him and say, "Talia has a job interview in Salt Lake City."

"Yikes. There might be a high school team there you could play for."

"You should focus on staying conscious on the crapper," I say. "We're too close to the playoffs for you to fuck around over that."

He pulls his crap cap out of his bag. "I'm wearing it for every shit, don't worry."

"At home, too. If you pass out there, the rats might eat your face off before you wake up."

He rolls his eyes. "I don't have rats in my house."

I pick up my phone so he knows I'm done with this conversation. I need to text Talia back, but it's hard to know what to say.

*Okay. When is the interview?*

*They need someone to start right away, so I'm flying there tomorrow and interviewing Wednesday morning.*

Fuck. I stare at the screen for a few seconds, trying to figure out what to say. I want her to find a job she loves, but I don't want it to be at the cost of us being together.

A better man would wish her luck. I'm too selfish

for that. But I don't want to say anything discouraging either, so I pretty much say nothing.

*I have to go, let's talk later.*

*Good luck tonight. Tell Isaac to wear his helmet, and tell Melina I stashed extra tape in the red bag. She'll know what it means.*

*I will. Miss you.*

The team is going back to our hotel for a pregame meal, and then I hope to get in a nap since I've been sleeping like shit.

It's hard to sleep when I finally found a woman I can see myself with forever, and I might lose her before we've really even gotten started.

# CHAPTER TWENTY-ONE

Talia

SALT LAKE CITY is sunny and cold today. From what little I've seen of it, it seems nice. My interview is over and I'm back at my hotel, packing for my afternoon flight back to Cleveland.

The job sounds perfect. It's funded privately, and there's a lot of money available that isn't even being spent. I could grow the program into something that really makes a difference, not just for the people served by it, but also by giving paid training and internships to college students who want to work with people who have disabilities.

I'd be a four-hour flight away from Cleveland, with a two-hour time difference. A long-distance relationship with Lucien would be possible, but not easy. If he even wanted that.

When I finish packing, I have about half an hour free before I have to leave for the airport. I sit down on the perfectly made bed, looking up clips from last night's game.

Lucien got an assist on a power play goal. I've already watched the clip of the team gathering to celebrate the goal, because his smile in it makes me mushy.

After Kyle broke up with me, I swore I'd be single for at least the next five years. I didn't want another relationship—especially with a hockey player. But then I met Lucien.

I didn't text him to tell him how the interview went, because I know he's secretly hoping this job won't work out. I like that he wants to be around me so much. If he was excited about the possibility of my moving to Salt Lake City, that would be a major red flag.

A text comes up on my phone screen, and I'm surprised when I see it's from Audra.

*Hey. Can we talk sometime?*

I'm shocked. The way we left things, I imagine she just wants to tell me to go fuck myself. But I'm curious, and I have time to kill, so I text back.

*Sure. Call me anytime.*

Within a minute, my phone rings, the call from an unknown number.

"Hello?"

"Hey, it's me," she says. "Thanks for letting me call."

A few seconds of silence pass before I say, "Is everything okay?"

She hums with amusement. "I got cussed out in Thai last night at dinner."

I pinch my brows together. "That's ... interesting."

Audra sighs softly. "The honeymoon was at a resort, and it's pretty secluded. We went to a little town about an hour away last night for dinner, and I guess the people who work there recognized us from all the social media stuff."

"Oh."

I could apologize, but I'm not going to. My terrible toast at the reception was the first time I called them both out about what happened. Maybe it wasn't the best time to do it, but if they had both handled things better before—or maybe, I don't know, *not cheated*—it never would have come to that. I didn't know how much I needed to say what I did until I had time to think about it.

"We couldn't figure out what was going on," she says. "One lady was yelling at us, and two other ladies were laughing and pointing. So I turned on

Google Translate and it didn't get everything, but when I saw 'bad sister' and 'you spank him,' I knew."

It's all I can do not to laugh, but I keep it in. "I don't know what to say, Audra. I didn't mean for that to happen."

She sighs, not saying anything for a few seconds. I hear a dinging sound in the background.

"I don't know why I had to travel across the world and have it yelled at me in Thai, but I know why she said it and I needed to tell you ... I am the bad sister. I deserved what you said. And more, really."

The genuine remorse in her tone softens something inside me. "I shouldn't have said it like that, though. Not at your wedding reception."

"You had some liquid courage. And that's on us for the open bar."

I laugh, and it gives me a pang, because I haven't laughed with my sister over anything in a long time.

"Well, we went viral, and not everyone can say that," I say.

"I can't even follow it anymore. People want me dead. Strangers behind keyboards are the cruelest people in the world."

"Stay away from it. I haven't looked at any of it since the day after it happened."

"It did lead to an interesting convo for me and

Kyle." There's a smile in her voice. "He's never asked me to spank him."

I cringe. "I don't know what to say here."

"It's okay. I just ... I was wrong. I wanted you back in my life so much that I pushed Mom and Dad to get you to the wedding, and then I pushed you over the dress and the photos. I should have let you do what was right for you, even if it meant you didn't come."

I'm too stunned to respond, but after a long pause, I say, "I appreciate that."

"I know too much has happened for me to even hope things could be like they used to. But I miss you, Talia. If you ever feel like we could talk again, even if it means we only talk on the phone and only about certain subjects, I'll take it."

I never imagined Audra saying anything like this. Especially now, when I embarrassed her and Kyle on a pretty much global scale.

"I'll think about it. And no matter what happens, I do still love you. If you truly needed something, I'd be there."

"I know." Her voice is choked with tears. "You're a better person than I am. You never would have done to me what I did to you."

"If I truly needed something, you'd be there."

"I would."

"Are you guys okay?" I ask. "Like, do you feel

safe? Because it really worries me that you said people want you dead."

"We're flying home now, and there are security people meeting us at the airport."

"That's ..." I sigh softly. "It's scary. I don't want anything bad to happen to you guys. I'd offer to help pay for the security, but I'm broke."

"Don't worry about it. Kyle's team is taking care of the cost of security for him, so we aren't paying for all of it."

"Be safe, okay?"

"I will. And before you go, I want you to know I'm so happy for you and Lucien. I know we'll never double date or anything, but ... maybe someday I could see the two of you by myself. Dinner or something. I can tell it's the real thing with you guys. He seems like a really good guy who has your back."

"He is and he does."

"I'll let you go. Thanks, Talia."

"Sure. Take care."

"You too."

I end the call and text Lucien.

*Wait until I tell you about the phone call I just got from Audra.*

He texts back right away.

*Lucien: Hit me. Is she suing you? She can bring that shit on because I've got a great attorney.*

*Talia: No, she pretty much apologized.*

*Lucien: For real? That call must've been long if she listed out everything she's done.*

*Talia: It wasn't super long. She said she gets why I said what I did, thanks to a Thai woman who sounds quite lovely.*

*Lucien: I want a full replay of the convo when I get home tomorrow. What time's your flight?*

*Talia: 3:45. I'm leaving for the airport soon.*

*Lucien: How did the interview go?*

*Talia: It was good.*

*Lucien: Hey, I love you. I don't want you to move, but I'm always rooting for you. Never against you. OK?*

*Talia: Thank you. I love you, too. I miss you so much.*

*Lucien: Carter and Suki invited us to fondue night tomorrow, but I passed. I want an evening of just us.*

*Talia: You turned down fondue on my behalf???*

*Lucien: Was that a mistake?*

*Talia: No, I'm kidding. But I do love fondue, so I expect you to make it up to me in bed tomorrow night.*

*Lucien: You got it, babe. I'm all yours.*

I smile, my stomach somersaulting as I read his words. Biting my lower lip, I send him a text.

*Talia: I have a crazy idea ...*

*Lucien: Does it involve my ass? I'm adventurous in bed, but I don't want to get cornholed.*

I laugh out loud and type out another message.

*Talia: It doesn't, but we're going to talk later about you bringing that up out of nowhere. I think you're using reverse psychology on me ... what if I change my flight from Cleveland to Vegas if I can? Think my dad would let me hitch a ride home on the team plane?*

*Lucien: I think that's a phenomenal idea. I'll pay for your flight.*

*Talia: You don't need to. My dad told me I can use his card for expenses until I'm back on my feet.*

*Lucien: No, seriously. Let me pay.*

*Talia: It might be expensive since it's last minute.*

*Lucien: It doesn't matter. If it means I get to see you tonight instead of tomorrow, do it.*

*Talia: Okay, thanks. Will you ask my dad to find me a seat for the game in the arena if possible?*

*Lucien: Yep. If you find a flight, text it to me and I'll pay for it.*

*Talia: Okay. I have to look now, so I can still make the Cleveland flight if I don't find one.*

*Lucien: Hopefully I'll see you tonight. I don't care what it costs, so don't consider that.*

*Talia: Okay. I'll try my best to find one.*

It only takes me about five minutes to find a flight departing at 4:10 with seats available. I text it to Lucien and he buys it immediately.

Tonight's not going to be a boring night on my dad's couch after all.

# CHAPTER TWENTY-TWO

Lucien

"Beaumont," Coach says, inclining his head toward the visiting coach's office space.

I was about to go do my pregame stretching, but I go into the office instead, where he's sitting at the desk, his hands steepled beneath his chin.

"Close the door," he says.

I do. Sitting down in the chair across from him, I ask, "Were you able to get it?"

He furrows his brow. "Get what?"

"A seat for Talia tonight."

"Oh, yeah. She's on the glass."

I relax. "Great. Thanks."

"I didn't do it for you, I did it for my daughter."

Fucking grouch. "Thanks for doing it for her."

He studies me for a few seconds, then asks, "Are you in love with Talia?"

This feels like a trick question. Like he's about to accuse me of doing something I didn't do.

"Yes, Coach."

"How many times have you been in love?"

"Um ... I don't know. Once, maybe? I thought I was in love, at least. But I was only nineteen. Life looked a lot different then."

"Why did that relationship end?"

"My travel schedule. She said I wasn't around enough, but it's not like I can pick and choose which games I go to."

"This job is hard on relationships."

I nod, wondering where he's going with this.

"How do you know you're in love with her?" he presses.

"Coach, are you ... looking for relationship advice?"

He laughs and scrubs a hand down his face. "Fuck no, and if I was, I wouldn't be asking you, Beaumont. Just answer the question."

I can't hesitate, and sure as hell can't mention anything sexual, but the only thing running through my mind is Isaac spitting out inappropriate answers to the question.

"She's my favorite person," I say, forcing Isaac's

face from my mind. "She's funny and sharp and she calls me out on my shit. I'd rather sit on the couch and watch a movie with her than go out with the guys. I'm not sleeping because I'm so wrecked over her job interview in Salt Lake City."

"What if you get tired of her after a month?"

"Coach, I don't get tired of Talia. We've spent a lot of time being together around the clock, and it just makes *not* being with her that much worse. She loves hockey and is so damn good at what she does that she's increased my range of motion."

"So you like that she's part of your world?"

I hesitate. "Sorry, that's making me think of *The Little Mermaid*."

He drops his brows, aggravated. "Stay on track, Beaumont. Did she say how the interview went?"

"Great, of course. Who wouldn't want to hire her? Some Mormon will probably be trying to make my girl his fourth wife by this time next week."

Coach ignores my comment. "I may have a way to keep her in Cleveland."

I lean forward slightly, waiting for him to say more.

"That would be great. What is it?"

He puts his hand up—his way of saying, *not so fast, I'm not done explaining.* I've seen this move many times.

"What matters most is what she wants. I'm not

going to try to pressure her into anything. If this Salt Lake City job ends up being what she wants, that's where she'll be going."

I shift in my seat, irritated. "What makes you think I want anyone to force her into anything? She's her own person, it's her decision."

"If she stays and then things go bad between you guys, that's gonna fall back on you. That's why I'm trying to find out how serious you are about her."

"I'm very serious. I'd never take advantage of your daughter. I was afraid to even touch her for a while, because—"

He gives me his palm again. "Don't ever mention you touching my daughter again, Beaumont. I would've put my entire foot up your ass already, but I like the way you took care of her in Hawaii. You must care about her to give up your break to be there with her. And then you stayed at Isaac's for a few days to keep her out of the spotlight."

"Did she tell you what a slob he is?"

Coach shakes his head. "No one needs to tell me. I imagine his house has the piano from the movie *Big*, a TV, a bunch of gumball machines, and nothing else."

"You're not far off."

He gives me a pointed look, putting his lower arms on the desk. "This stays between you and me only. Are we clear?"

"Yes, Coach. It won't leave this room."

"Isaac and Melina went to McClain and made the case for us to create a team position for Talia. She wouldn't be Melina's assistant, but they'd work together. Melina would pass some of her duties on to Talia, and they'd work together to create some new work for her."

I didn't even think this was an option. Not only could Talia stay in Cleveland, but she could stay with the team. It's a great idea, because she's good at what she does and would be an asset to the team, and she and I could still be together.

"I take back what I said about Isaac being a slob. I can't believe he and Melina did that."

"Melina asked me if it was okay first. I told her I can't be a part of asking our team owner to create a job for my daughter, but I wasn't going to stop her from doing it. She and Isaac got it done."

"That's great news. When can we tell Talia?"

He sits back in his chair. "This isn't the type of work she wants to do, Beaumont. She wants to help people with disabilities be physically active."

I deflate because he's right.

"Okay, so then ... what's next?"

"Hunter Beck."

I pinch my brows together, confused about what Pittsburgh's billionaire team captain has to do with Talia.

Coach continues. "It wouldn't be appropriate for me to approach Beck and ask him to seed the money for a league-wide foundation that connects every team with disabled people in their communities. To provide equipment and help in getting youth wheelchair hockey programs and field hockey programs going. Where players could show up to help coach and cheer on the participants."

My jaw drops. "Holy shit! Talia had an idea for something like that here in Cleveland."

Coach shrugs a shoulder. "Like I said, it wouldn't be appropriate for me to try to get that going. But if another player were to ask Beck, he'd be ready to write that check. And then we'd need someone on our staff to run the program, and ..."

"Talia's perfect for it."

My throat tightens with emotion. He did this. It's a done deal, and he's telling me I just need to place a call to Beck so the idea comes from me and not him. It's a perfect scenario.

"I'm ... damn close to speechless, Coach," I say. "Thank you."

"I didn't do it for you, I did it for Talia."

"I know, but—"

He cuts me off with the palm. "I wasn't done, Beaumont. It's for Talia because I selfishly want to keep her close, but also because you're the kind of man I always wanted for her. You're ten times the man Kyle Macintire is and I'd be proud to call you my son-in-law one day."

My throat tightens even further. Coach doesn't dole out personal compliments, and I'm stunned by what he just said.

"Thank you, Coach. I won't let you down."

"This is your last chance to tell me if you're not serious about her. I can kill this job offer without her ever knowing. And I want to do that if you aren't one hundred percent certain you want to be with her a year from now—and ten years from now. If so, let her go to Salt Lake City and start fresh."

I shake my head. "I'm very serious about her. I love her. It made my entire fucking day that she decided to come here tonight instead of going back to Cleveland."

"Good. I'll make sure Melina has a double room so Talia can stay with her."

I freeze for a second, then say, "Seriously?"

He gives me another irritated look. "She's my daughter. As far as I'm concerned, she'll be staying in Melina's room. Am I going to drop by at midnight and make sure she's there? No, but don't say anything—ever—to make me think she was anywhere else tonight. I imagine the team will pay for rooms for her that are empty a lot if she joins the team, but I sure as fuck don't want anyone confirming it."

I nod. "I understand, Coach. Thank you."

"Get out of here. And let me be the one to make the offer to Talia. This conversation never happened."

"Understood, Coach."

I leave the office, finally able to relax and be happy about this idea. Hopefully she'll want the job. I think she will, but I won't fully relax until she tells me she's taking the job and staying with the team. And, more importantly, with me.

# CHAPTER TWENTY-THREE

Talia

Two Weeks Later

Suki snort-laughs as she looks inside the box of the gift she just opened. "Oh my gosh. This is amazing."

The baby shower Mara is hosting for her is so big it's being held at Harry's restaurant. Harry closed it for the day and transformed it into a dreamy space with a "Twinkle Twinkle Little Star" theme. I helped Dex figure out how to attach our fake clouds to the ceiling without ruining it. Alcohol was involved, but I stopped myself at one drink.

When Suki pulls out a giant gray T-shirt and shows us all what it says, the whole room bursts into laughter. It says "Big Brother," and it's for Darling.

The team's gift to Suki and Carter is thirty thousand dollars in stocks for their baby, a designer stroller, a sweater for the baby with Carter's name and number, and matching shirts they had made for the girls and Darling. It won't be easy to get a good photo of everyone since the girls' shirts say "Big Sister" on the front and Darling's wording is on his back, but I have a feeling Suki will figure something out. She's the creative maven who hosts parties and chooses milestone gifts for everyone else, so she deserves a lavish shower for her family.

"Need another one?" Lucien asks from next to me, taking my empty glass.

"Sure."

"Dr Pepper?"

I nod. Lainey has really turned me on to drinking Dr Pepper. Since I started my new job with the team, I've been bringing cans of it with me on the team plane, and the attendants told me to stop because it's their job to make sure we have everything we could want or need when traveling.

That's a hard thing to adjust to. Being an official staff member of the team means details are taken care of, so I can focus on my job.

It's been a whirlwind. I've had several video

meetings with Hunter Beck, the billionaire team captain who's funding the new program. He's letting me take the lead, and so far has been willing to fund it at a level that's a dream come true.

Between my work with the team and creating the new program, I'm spread thin, so I'm staying at Lucien's instead of my dad's. I went from thinking I might have to move several states away to being his live-in girlfriend pretty much overnight.

It's good, though. Really good. We have a routine when we're home: he makes the coffee and does all the dishes, I order the groceries and do all the laundry. Both of us stay in motion until seven p.m. when we're home. That's the cutoff time for any kind of work.

We spend a lot of our evenings alone together, still in that blissful new-relationship cocoon. But we also spend time with our friends, who feel more like family.

Suki opens the next gift, which is a card. She reads it, her eyes widening as she looks up, scanning the faces in the room.

"This is ... wow, I don't even know what to say," she says, tears shining in her eyes.

Her eyes lock with Carter's and he walks over to read the card. His lips part with surprise and he starts scanning the room, too.

"Coach? Are you here?"

"I'm here."

My dad calls out from the back of the room, and I do a double take when I see the woman at the table next to his. They're both sitting at tables with one side chairs and the other side a booth, and she's scooted over so far she's practically in his lap.

When everyone turns to look, she scoots a few inches away. I exchange a look with Lucien because she looks *my fucking age*, and she was clearly cozying up to my dad.

Lucien purses his lips and looks away, wanting nothing to do with my questioning look. He's going to hear about her later, though. Bet.

"Coach is giving us a trip," Suki says. "An incredibly generous one. Thank you, Noel."

She sets the card down and gets up, her belly making her a little slower. Making her way through the tables filled with people, she reaches my father, who is standing up by then. Carter follows her.

When she hugs my dad, she's clearly emotional, and Carter is, too. My heart swells. I would've missed things like this if I'd moved. Though I would've missed Lucien most of all, being part of my dad's Crush family is very important to me now.

Here, I'm not the woman whose sister stole her fiancé. I'm not the depressed woman who could hardly get off her couch for months. I'm not the drunken girl from the viral video.

I'm a team trainer. Lucien's girlfriend. Suki, Mara and Lainey's friend. The head coach's daughter. But none of the other things are because I'm his daughter. I have my own place here, and I'm happier than I've ever been.

Lucien returns to his seat, hands me my drink, and then leans over and whispers in my ear. I turn to whisper back.

"A week at an Italian villa with a yacht. But don't repeat that. If they tell people, it's fine, but we're not going to."

He nods, looking impressed, and mutters, "Damn, Coach."

Angie got a lot of my dad's money in the divorce, but he still has more than enough. He invested a lot when he was a player, and those investments have paid off many times over. He invited me and Lucien on a two-week summer trip to the South of France, and my younger siblings, Chance and Chloe, are also going.

I've been on those trips before, and they're unforgettable. We'll mostly be on a yacht, hosting parties and going to parties on other yachts. And we'll also explore on land and do some shopping.

Audra and Kyle weren't invited, even though I told my dad I didn't mind if he invited them. He said being trapped on a boat with Kyle and Lucien at the same time isn't really a vacation for him.

Which, fair. After all the wedding antics, I'm sure one or both of them would end up being thrown overboard at least once. Dad's not a Kyle fan, for obvious reasons, but he likes Lucien. He just doesn't want to be seen as giving him preferential treatment, so he treats him like all his other players.

Suki is back to opening gifts, and I turn to look at my dad again. The woman is sitting close to him again, laughing. Dad's lips are quirking with a smile. I furrow my brow with disapproval.

She's way too young for him. He's still newly divorced—it hasn't even been a year yet. But she's gazing adoringly at him, like she wants him to put a baby in her immediately.

I lean closer to Lucien. "Look at the fetus flirting with my dad."

"I saw."

That makes me smile. He refuses to look again, because he doesn't want me to think he's gawking at another woman.

"How old do you think she is?"

He gives me a neutral look, keeping his voice soft. "I think we should talk about that later."

Suki finishes opening all the gifts, and Harry's servers start to bring out dessert plates. He made a delicious lunch of cucumber and cream cheese sandwiches, smoked salmon sandwiches, and salad. He's also serving individual lemon tarts, in keeping with the yellow color scheme, since Suki and Carter decided not to find out their baby's gender until it's born.

The tarts even have powdered sugar stars dusted on top. Lucien only has two bites of his before pushing the plate aside.

"It's amazing," he says, setting his fork down. "I wasn't going to have any, but then I saw it and I had to."

He's on a no-sugar diet in the home stretch of the hockey season. The team is in a tight race for a playoff spot, so the players have all tightened up their diets and training routines.

I get to be on the team bench during games now, and it's my favorite part of the job. Melina and I go out on the ice to assess injuries, and we bandage cuts and check injuries for players who are on the bench.

Even though I'm not a player, I feel like part of the game now. A Nashville player came tumbling over the wall onto our bench last week, and even though Silas blocked him from landing right on top of me, a bead of his sweat still splashed onto my arm.

I get to be front and center for the chirping between players now, and I see why Lucien's teammates sometimes call him Loki. He's an instigator, throwing opponents off their game as often as he can.

The shower is wrapping up, people starting to leave, when Lainey approaches me.

"Hey, are you free for some shopping sometime? I have to get a swimsuit for our trip and I'd rather do literally anything else. Maybe we could make it fun somehow. Like not shop for swimsuits and go out to eat instead."

She and Bash are taking a trip to Fiji in the offseason, and she's pretending she's excited about it to him, but secretly she's freaking out about wearing a swimsuit the entire time, her very fair skin getting crisped in the sun, and the possibility that the water there will give her an IBS flare.

"I'd love that," I say. "I need to buy a couple suits myself for our trip."

"Sunday?"

"I can't do it that day. Lucien's sister and brother-in-law are coming to visit." I mentally consider my schedule. "What about Wednesday afternoon?"

"I might be working. I'll check my schedule and send you some options for dates."

"Perfect."

Lucien recently told me the full extent of his sister's battle with cancer. She'd just found out she was pregnant when she was diagnosed with the same kind of breast cancer that killed their mother. After many conversations with her husband and medical team, she and her husband made the agonizing decision to end the pregnancy.

I'm excited about meeting her. She's been cancer-free for eight months. Their visit will just be for the weekend, but we're going to make the most of it. We have a dinner reservation at Harry's restaurant Friday night and a home game Saturday night.

Suki hugs me when Lucien and I tell her we're leaving.

"This was so beautiful," she says. "Thank you for everything you did."

"You deserve it. And it was mostly Mara and Harry."

She stands back and cups my face in her hands. "I haven't gotten a chance to say welcome to the family. You already felt like part of it, but officially. Carter says you're a huge asset to the team."

Before, I would have made that into a quip about having a huge ass. But Lucien has taught me—through endless compliments—not to put myself down anymore.

"Thank you. I love everyone I work with."

"I'll need a few weeks after the baby is born, but then the girls and I want to be part of the new thing you're doing to help the team connect with people who have disabilities. Whatever you need."

"Really? Because I'm looking for team ambassadors. One of the things we're doing is giving away seats at every home game to people with disabilities and their caregivers, and I want them to have someone to show them around the arena and make sure they're taken care of."

She smiles brightly. "We would love that."

"Great. Let's talk more about it at the next foundation meeting."

Lucien hugs her and says, "Keep that bun in the oven for another few weeks, okay?"

She laughs. "I'm going to try. If you guys make it to the championship, it might get a little dicey."

Of course, Carter wants to be there for the birth of their child, but it would be hard for the team to lose him during a championship run. Family first, though. Everyone on the team, including my dad, believes in that.

"Are we going home?" Lucien asks as we walk out of the restaurant.

"Yes, it's going to be an early night for me."

I love traveling with the team, but it's exhausting. Flying out in the middle of the night. Getting to hotels before sunrise. And a boyfriend who's still running on game adrenaline after games and loves to fuck his way to sleepiness.

Not that I'm complaining. I've never had so many orgasms, and he always puts me before himself in bed.

"Anything you need me to do before we leave tomorrow?" he asks.

"Will you get me some Sour Patch Kids?"

"Yep. Is that it?"

"Oh crap, I'm going to need tampons."

"I got you. Just send me a picture of the box."

We're leaving early tomorrow for Vancouver—the first game against Kyle's team since the wedding. I'm not stressed about it, though. The entire internet is talking about this matchup and planning to watch with popcorn, and I'm sure Lucien will make it worth their while.

And even though I don't care what happens to Kyle anymore, I won't complain about having a front-row seat while my man beats his ass.

# CHAPTER TWENTY-FOUR

Lucien

Three Months Later

"How was she?" Suki whispers, setting her bag down on a side table.

"Absolutely perfect." Talia gazes down at the sleeping bundle in her arms.

She and I babysat Carter and Suki's six-week-old daughter while they went out for dinner. The other three girls are spending the night with Leo and Mara, who are taking them swimming and bowling.

Rachel Amelia Stanton arrived in the middle of the night, all of us showing up to the hospital with no regard for visiting hours. I got emotional when Carter brought her out of the hospital nursery to show her to us, tears shining in his eyes when he told us her name.

They named her after his late sister. She had Carter wrapped around her tiny little finger from the moment he saw her.

I've never been around babies, and I had no idea how loud they could scream. Rachel started crying so hard I thought my eardrums would split about an hour after Carter and Suki left. I was ready to call 911, honestly, but Talia had me hold her and walk around the kitchen while she warmed up a bottle of breast milk.

As soon as Talia put the bottle up to her mouth, she went quiet and started guzzling it like a frat boy shotgunning a beer. I was worried she wasn't even breathing because she was so consumed with drinking the bottle.

Talia carried her around and patted her back until a lumberjack-sized burp came out of her, and then did some baby massage on her. We haven't talked about kids any more specifically than saying we both want them someday, but when she took a picture of me holding Rachel, I could tell she was thinking about it.

We need to get married first. I'd marry her today, but Coach wouldn't like that. He wants us to be together for at least a year before I propose, and I respect that. We've been spending a lot of time with him in the offseason. Having him over for dinner, going to the farmers' market and biking local trails.

"Daddy's here now." Carter gently takes his daughter from Talia. "Hey there, peanut, you're awake."

"How was dinner?" Talia asks Suki.

"Amazing. I had the best steak."

"We can keep hanging with Rachel if you guys need to do anything else."

Suki sits down in a recliner, looking relaxed. "Thanks, but we're good. We still have a freezer full of food people have brought and we don't stress about the house being clean."

Darling spent most of the evening sleeping on one end of the couch. He snores so loud he wakes himself up. After lifting his head to look around, he drops it back down and returns to sleeping.

"He's wiped out," I say. "Is he okay?"

"Hallie played with him a lot in the yard earlier," Carter says. "Now he'll sleep until he wants to eat."

"And come into our bedroom at three a.m. when we're finally getting some sleep to wake us up and let us know he's hungry," Suki says.

"What does he think of the baby?" I ask.

"He sniffs her a lot, but he's mostly not interested in her. He leaves the room when she's crying."

"So do I," Carter quips.

"Yeah, right." Suki laughs. "I lose more sleep to breastfeeding, so Carter gets to change the atomic waste blowout diapers."

"It's the most disgusting thing imaginable," he says. "It makes me regret being born with a sense of smell."

"She can't help it," Talia says, laughing.

"Aren't you guys leaving for your trip tomorrow?" Suki asks.

Talia grins. "Yes. Our bags are packed and we're so ready to go."

Coach is picking us up in the morning to go to the airport. Chase and Chloe are already with him. It's his first vacation with them since the divorce, and he carved out some time to do things alone with each of them.

After we get back from this trip, we're meeting my dad in Maine for another one. He's never been there, so we're taking him to do some stuff. Lighthouses, lobsters, and a visit to Acadia National Park. Talia has it all planned out.

"I guess we'll get out of your hair, then," Lucien says, looking at me.

"Thanks, guys." Carter passes Rachel to Suki and walks us to the door. "Let's do a cookout when you finish traveling."

He hugs us both, slapping my back, then grins at

me, his hand on my upper arm. "Enjoy the South of France, man. It's all glamour and sun for now, but your diaper changing days will be here soon enough."

"I don't mind. We get enough travel in, you know? I'm looking forward to peaceful summers at home with my family. I think we both are."

I look at Talia, who nods. "Definitely."

"What is this peace you speak of?" Suki quips. "We spend a lot of time mediating teenage girl arguments and prying nonedible objects from a pig's mouth."

"And cleaning up toilets that overflowed. Because if it doesn't flush the first four times, maybe it just needs a fifth, right?" Carter says.

"That too." Suki walks over to us. "And then mediating another teenage girl fight about who clogged the toilet."

"Can't wait!" I say, taking Talia's hand as we walk out the front door. "Take care, guys."

When we get back to the car, Talia gives me a questioning look. "So that didn't scare you away from having our own babies?"

"Nope. We'll figure it out." I start the car and begin our drive home. "And speaking of activities that lead to babies, I really hope you're in the mood."

"Why is that?" she asks, her tone teasing.

"Because I can't exactly rail you while we're

trapped on a boat with your dad. We need to get it in while we can."

"You've never had a problem getting it in, babe."

I scoff, laughing. "Goddamn right."

"Lucien?"

I look over at her.

"I love that a crying baby is scary to you and that you always laugh at my jokes. And that you lick my pussy like it's your job."

I grin at her. "It is my job, babe. I play hockey on the side, but licking your pussy is my primary vocation."

"Let's keep it that way for at least the next six decades."

"Believe me, I plan to."

I bring her hand to my lips and kiss the back of it. When she smiles back at me, I don't just see the smile of my beautiful best friend and girlfriend. It's the smile of my future wife. The mother of my future children. The smile I can't imagine ever being without.

# EPILOGUE

Noel

"I was so sorry to hear about you and Angie, Noel." Vivian Davis puts her hand on my forearm, running it slowly upward. "Oh wow, I didn't know a forearm could be so strong."

I sigh inwardly, missing the quiet comfort of my home, where I don't have to fend off divorcées and fortune seekers several times a day.

This trip has been fantastic. I needed the time to focus just on my kids. The divorce was tough for Chase and Chloe, and they've missed me since I moved out.

I've missed them too. My kids are everything to me. Even Audra, though our relationship is strained. I'm not angry at her, but if I could get away with it, I'd choke the life out of her husband. He's a punk who took advantage of not just one, but two of my daughters. Their relationship will never be the same. Kyle Macintire is nothing to me but Audra's partner. I'll never call him my son-in-law.

Lucien, on the other hand, is well on his way. He makes Talia happier than I've ever seen her. The glow she has isn't just from all the sun she's gotten on this trip. It's also from the confidence and happiness she's found in a relationship with Lucien.

I never would've imagined them together. He's a menace on the ice, telling our opponents he fucks their mothers in ways that would make a sailor blush. Lucien's not just a great defender—he's also my highest scoring one.

I've gotten to know him better on this trip. He took Chase out for a day of jet skiing and parasailing so I could take Talia and Chloe shopping. Chase basks in his attention; Lucien is like an older brother to him already.

At age forty-seven, my jet skiing days are behind me. I'd rather relax on the yacht's deck with a drink and watch the sunset.

Talia comes over to me and Vivian, saving me from small talk with her.

"Dad, can you come help me with something?"

"Yeah, no problem." I nod at Vivian. "Enjoy the rest of your trip."

"I hope to see you again."

I hope *not* to see her again, so I just offer a polite smile. The market must be rough out there for single fortysomething women, because I've gotten everything from mild flirting to a note with a phone number and an offer to suck my dick on this trip. Which is pretty gross when you consider I'm here with my kids.

"Jesus, why are women so thirsty?" Talia says under her breath. "I thought she was going to take off her bikini top and show you the goods."

"Thanks for the save."

Talia is the most disgusted of all my kids about women showing their interest in me. Chloe thinks it's weird and Chase thinks it's cool. Talia always has the strongest reaction, though.

"She was practically drooling. Does she have any self-respect?"

"Don't pay any attention to it, Tally. I'm not interested in anything. Nothing casual, nothing serious, and nothing in between. I've had my fill of relationships."

She flicks a glance at me, trying to make sure I'm telling the truth. I don't know why—we've had this conversation several times and I've never changed my mind.

My life now is my kids, coaching hockey, and keeping up with a few close friends. I plan to travel as much as I can in my offseason. Angie only cared about being seen by famous and wealthy people when we traveled. I couldn't give a shit about that. I want to visit rainforests, see icebergs, and eat food from as many countries as I can.

Hockey has been at the forefront of my life for twenty-eight years now. I played as a pro for fifteen years, going into coaching as soon as I retired. The grind is pretty similar either way, but coaching doesn't take the same toll on my body that playing did.

"Want to do dinner in the dining room we've been using?" Talia asks. "I like that it's private."

I nod because I like that, too. My kids have enjoyed this trip, and we only have three more days here. We're going inland tomorrow for sightseeing and a dinner reservation in Saint-Tropez. It's always been a favorite place to eat when we travel here.

Chase and Chloe are spending another couple weeks with me back in Cleveland, and when they leave, I'll start preparing for my upcoming season.

Angie always said I'm married to hockey, and I'm fine with that. Hockey can't cheat on me with the contractor and clean me out in a divorce. From now on, I'm staying single.

# WANT MORE?

The next book in the Love on the Line series is Crushing on the Coach.

Book 7 - Jonah

Book 8 - Kit

Book 9 - Olivier

**Colorado Coyotes Series**

Book 1 - The Donor

Book 2 - The Opponent

Book 3 - The Proposal

Book 4 - The Imposter

Book 5 - The Face-Off

**Sin city saints Series**

Book 1 - Maverick

Book 2 - Pike

Book 3 - Pax

**St. Lous Mavericks series**

Book 1 - Hard Fall

Book 2 - Hard Limit

Book 3 - Hard Pass

Book 4 - Hard Luck

Book 5 - Hard Hit

**Fire on Ice Series**

Book 1 - Bound

Book 2 - Captive

Book 3 - Edge

Book 4 - Drive

Book 5 - Release

## On the Line Series

Book 1 - Killian

Book 2 - Bennett

## Lockhart Brothers Series

Book 1 - Deep Down

Book 2 - In Deep

Book 3 - Drawn Deeper

Book 4 - Hidden Depth

## Filthy Series

Book 1 - Dirty Work

Book 2 - Dirty Secret

Book 3 - Dirty Defiance

## Standalones

Come Closer

Buried

Sweet Sixteen

His

Alpha Mail

Healing Touch

Barely Breathing

Exiled

Unspoken

# ABOUT THE AUTHOR

Brenda Rothert lives in Central Illinois with her husband, children and three dogs. She loves to hear from readers through her website or her Facebook Group, Rothert's Readers.

Keep up with all the latest on Brenda's books and get bonus content by signing up for her newsletter at her website, brendarothert.com.